# HONEYMOON
## Ellen James

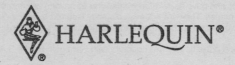

HARLEQUIN®

TORONTO • NEW YORK • LONDON
AMSTERDAM • PARIS • SYDNEY • HAMBURG
STOCKHOLM • ATHENS • TOKYO • MILAN • MADRID
PRAGUE • WARSAW • BUDAPEST • AUCKLAND

ISBN 0-373-70799-1

HONEYMOON

**Printed in U.S.A.**

# HONEYMOON

# CHAPTER ONE

"DON'T FORGET TO TALK about us while we're gone!"

With these words, Jackie Shaw whirled onto the dance floor in the arms of her fiancé. And that left Jackie's sister Toni facing a handsome stranger at the dinner table.

Toni generally felt one of two emotions for her sister: affection and exasperation. At the moment exasperation had the upper hand. Toni had arrived at this chic San Francisco restaurant expressly at Jackie's invitation—yet Jackie had deserted her without even bothering to make introductions. Hence the handsome stranger. Hence the fact that Toni didn't have a clue as to the man's identity.

He didn't help her out. He merely stood there, gazing at her with an unreadable expression in his dark brown eyes. His hair was a luxuriant shade of russet and his features—although currently rather stern—combined for a most pleasing effect...well-defined nose, strong jaw. His wool jacket was a wonderful soft shade of gray. The man apparently had it all...good looks *and* good taste.

Toni stuck out her hand. "Antonia Shaw."

He shook her hand firmly. "Kyle Brennan."

"Sister of the intended bride," she said.

He smiled. "Best friend of the intended groom."

"I suppose we're here to offer our congratulations," Toni said.

He nodded gravely. Then he pulled out a chair for her and she sat down. He sat across from her. The surroundings were lovely: the candlelight sparkling on fine china, the gilded woodwork, the string quartet elegant in black tie, the panoramic view of glittering nighttime San Francisco.

Toni's gaze strayed back to Kyle Brennan. He really was attractive. Certainly it had something to do with his looks and his tall, rangy physique. Even more, it had something to do with an underplayed suggestion of power. Toni had already sensed a few women in the restaurant giving Kyle Brennan surreptitious glances. She couldn't blame them—he was the type of man who drew the eye.

It seemed he was also the type of man who had only to lift his hand for a waiter to materialize.

"What would you like to drink?" Kyle asked.

She ordered a rum cocktail, and Kyle ordered a brandy. Then Toni gazed at Jackie and fiancé as they danced by, wrapped in each other's arms.

"At least, I'm assuming that's Jackie's fiancé," she said wryly. "Since I haven't been introduced yet..."

"You haven't met Hollan before this?" Kyle sounded surprised.

"I didn't even know his name was Hollan. Jackie rang me up this morning, out of the blue, and announced she was engaged to be married. She said she wanted me to meet the lucky man tonight—so here I am. Straight from work."

Kyle looked thoughtful. "Maybe you should talk to your sister more often. They've been engaged for two months."

"You're kidding."

"Afraid not."

Toni shook her head in disbelief. Whenever there'd been a new man in Jackie's life, she would call Toni at all hours to rehash every tortuous romantic detail. It wasn't like Jackie to keep secrets—she far preferred others to share the drama of her life.

"Jackie usually confides everything to me," Toni said. "In fact, she often confides more than I want to know."

Jackie and Hollan danced dreamily by once more. Toni struggled with new emotions. Perhaps she'd grown too accustomed to fulfilling the role of Jackie's confidante—the older, wiser sister. Okay, maybe not that much older; only eighteen months separated her and Jackie. But Jackie often *seemed* so young, so in need of help and advice and a shoulder to cry on.

"I can't believe she neglected to tell me this little

detail," Toni murmured. She gazed long and hard at Kyle Brennan, as if he might actually have some insights into her sister's new behavior. But no answer was forthcoming.

She was relieved when the drinks came, offering a welcome distraction. She sipped her cocktail, the rum warming her throat. The string quartet had gone from playing a slow, nostalgic number to something with a distinctive modern beat. Out on the dance floor, Jackie and Hollan rose to the occasion. Jackie executed a twirl, then glided effortlessly back into her fiancé's arms. Hollan took her into a dip, allowing her long golden hair to brush the floor, while a smattering of applause came from the nearby tables. Toni, if she'd tried that move, would no doubt have landed on her rear end. It was the sort of contrast that had been set early in her relationship with her sister: Jackie was the graceful one, Toni the bookish one; Jackie the drama queen, Toni the straight-A scholar.

Kyle Brennan seemed absorbed by his own thoughts, but then he stirred. "What was the first thing you noticed when you came into this room?" he asked.

Toni drew her eyebrows together. "Mr. Brennan, I'm not in the mood for a game right now—"

"It's Kyle. But just answer the question, Antonia. What was the first thing you noticed when you came in?"

*You,* she could have said. *You were the first thing I noticed.* But she didn't think she should say this out loud. She had no business getting carried away by the man's attractiveness.

"I noticed... I don't know. The musicians. But what's the point of this—?"

"I'll tell you the first thing I noticed," he said seriously. "The cornice up there...see?"

Toni craned her neck and peered in the direction he'd indicated. She saw the ornate molding that ran all along the top of the wall.

"That," he said, "is the real thing—master plasterwork. See the intricacy of the design, the attention to detail? Small, important details...you lose touch with those when you design one more office building for one more client who only cares what kind of view there'll be in the corner suite." He spoke almost as if to himself.

"Let me guess," Toni said. "You wouldn't be an architect, by any chance?"

"I like to call myself one, anyway." Now he gave her a real smile. There ought to be a city ordinance against a man who could turn a smile like that on you.

A chirping came from Toni's briefcase. She unbuckled it and took out her cell phone. "Excuse me," she told Kyle, then put the phone to her ear. "Toni Shaw."

"Toni...what's happening? What's he like? You're

at the restaurant, aren't you?'' These words were spoken in something of a theatrical whisper.

Toni turned away just a bit from Kyle. ''Mom...I told you I'd call as soon as I had a chance.''

''I couldn't take the suspense any longer. Just tell me what he's like. You can talk, can't you?''

Toni glanced over at Kyle. He gazed out at the dance floor, seemingly making an effort not to listen.

''Mom,'' she said in a low voice. ''This isn't a good time. I haven't really met him yet, and—''

''He's *there,* isn't he?''

''He and Jackie are dancing,'' Toni said as patiently as possible.

''There must be something you can tell me about him. Jackie's never sprung an engagement on us before. Well, except for that time in the Bahamas, but I don't suppose that really counts.''

Toni knew all about the time in the Bahamas. Jackie had been engaged for a total of nine days, to a man she'd known for ten days. ''Mom,'' Toni said, ''I have to hang up now.''

''Can you at least tell me his name?''

''Hollan.''

''Holland? What kind of name is that?''

''Not Holland,'' Toni said. ''Hollan.''

''Hollan Nash the Third,'' Kyle supplied helpfully.

''Who's that talking?'' Toni's mother asked with interest.

"It's Hollan's friend. And if you want the name in full, it's Hollan Nash the Third."

"You say his friend is there?" her mother asked. "What kind of friend?"

Toni clenched her fingers around the phone. "I don't know a thing about *him,* except that he's an architect."

Kyle leaned toward the phone. "Hollan's an architect, too," he said.

"Mom, did you get that?" Toni asked dryly.

"Toni, ask his friend for details," her mother instructed.

"Mom, I *will* call you back." With a jab of her finger, Toni broke the connection and stuffed the phone back into her briefcase. "Uh...sorry about that," she told Kyle.

"Guess your mother didn't know about the engagement, either."

"Jackie didn't tell any of us about it till this morning," Toni said briskly. "Now, where were we?"

He gave her that smile again. "We were letting the conversation take us wherever it led."

She wanted to look away. She gazed into his dark brown eyes, seeing the glint of humor there, and knew she ought to look away. "Mr. Brennan—"

"Kyle, remember? And you're Antonia."

"Most people call me Toni," she said determinedly.

"I like Antonia better."

She reminded herself why she was here. "I think we should flag Jackie down. Then I can get to know Hollan, and then—"

"Then you can report back to your mother," Kyle said solemnly.

"You're having a good time with this, aren't you?" Toni muttered.

"The evening picked up the minute you arrived, Antonia."

She took another sip of her drink. "Let's stick to Jackie, all right? It's understandable that my mother's concerned. As far as men, go, Jackie tends to act on impulse. And that means sometimes she gets involved with men who just aren't...trustworthy."

"I see," Kyle said. "And your mother wants to know if Hollan is trustworthy."

"That's the upshot," Toni said. "Except I'm sure Mom finds all of this fascinating, too. That's the thing about Jackie. She does such reckless, unexpected things that you can't help being fascinated." It had been that way for as long as Toni could remember. Jackie had always been the one who kept her parents up late, worrying. She commanded their attention in ways Toni had never seemed able to do. Once, when Toni was a teenager, she'd protested. "Mom," she'd asked, "why don't you love me as much as Jackie?" Marianne Shaw had been startled. "But, honey," she'd answered, "of course I love you every bit as much. You're the one I can count on.'' The answer hadn't quite satisfied Toni.

"Anyway," Toni said now, "it really is time for me to meet Hollan, and welcome him into the family, I suppose.''

"There's no rush,'' Kyle said. "We're having a good time, aren't we?''

"I don't know—you tell me.''

"I'll admit that at first I wasn't enthusiastic about coming here tonight. 'Meet the bride's sister,' Hollan said. 'Nothing doing,' I said. 'You've tried to fix me up too many times before, and look how it's always turned out—'''

"Wait a minute," Toni interrupted. "Are you telling me this is…a setup? That's why Jackie and Hollan have left us here alone?''

"Take a look at them," Kyle said. "They're so caught up in each other they've forgotten about everything else—including you and me. But Hollan does have this habit of trying to fix me up. And if it turns out he saw tonight as just one more opportunity… I'm definitely not complaining.'' He sounded completely sincere, but that glint of humor never seemed to leave his eyes. And there it was…that smile of his. It warmed his face. It was certainly warming Toni. She had to do something about the situation immediately.

"If this really is a setup, it's a little awkward,'' she said. "Because I'm seeing someone. Jackie knows about me and Dan. I don't understand why she didn't mention it.'' Toni found it was a relief to bring this out in the open. She'd been sitting here, noticing Kyle Brennan far too much.

"I'd even hoped Dan could be here tonight,'' she said. "Dan Greene, my…'' Her voice trailed off. What *was* the proper term? Her current steady? Significant other? Boyfriend? None of those expressions seemed to fit. "Anyway,'' she went on, "I really wanted him to be here tonight. It's just that…he had a previous appointment.''

Kyle nodded impassively this time. Toni took another sip of her cocktail.

"Dan's playing basketball,'' she said almost defensively. "Friday's always his basketball night.'' Just as Wednesday was always movie night, and Saturday was always hang-out-at-the-local-bar-and-grill night. Somehow she suspected Kyle Brennan wasn't the kind of man who did something predictable every day of the week.

"I'm very happy with Dan,'' she added. And just then her briefcase chirped again.

She took the phone out and pressed it to her ear. "Hello.''

"You didn't call back.''

"Mom, it hasn't been ten *minutes*—''

"What did you find out?''

Toni stifled a groan. "Nothing. They're still dancing. And I still haven't met him."

"What about the friend? Couldn't he tell you anything?"

Toni glanced at Kyle. "Mom," she said. "I'll give
you a full report as soon as I can."

"I don't see how. You haven't made any progress
so far."

Toni sighed.

"Maybe I can help," Kyle said. He put out his hand
as if to take the phone.

"You can't be serious," Toni said. Could this situation get any more ridiculous? But then, with a shrug,
Toni handed the phone to Kyle. He settled back in his
chair with it.

"Mrs. Shaw, this is Kyle Brennan...just fine,
thanks. And you? Glad to hear it. I'm Hollan's business partner. Yes...an architectural firm...what's that?
Hmm...yes, I'd say we've done pretty well for ourselves."

Already Toni regretted letting her mother loose on
Kyle. She gestured for him to return the phone, but he
only settled back more comfortably.

"As a matter of fact," he said, "Hollan and I go
way back. College swim team...absolutely. He's an
excellent swimmer. Me...? I don't compete anymore.
But maybe you can answer a question. Your daughter

Toni says she's seeing someone. Comes as something of a disappointment. Guy name of Dan…''

Toni gestured emphatically this time. Kyle ignored her. "Is that so," he commented into the phone. "A banker…nice fellow? Plays basketball, too, I understand…that's interesting…I've enjoyed talking to you, too, Mrs. Shaw…goodbye."

He handed the phone over. Toni grabbed it, switched it off and stuffed it into her briefcase. "Are you pretty much done amusing yourself?" she asked caustically.

"Your mom says Dan Greene works in your dad's bank. A member of the board, no less."

"I *know* where he works—"

"Your mother says you're involved with this guy because he's the safe type. She says you've been hurt before, and that's why you've picked safe."

Toni felt herself flush. She couldn't believe it. "Kyle, I know this is highly entertaining for you. Do you behave this way with every woman you meet, or am I just lucky?"

He appeared grave once more. "You're just lucky, I guess."

Toni suspected that Kyle Brennan could charm any woman with scarcely half an effort. He'd obviously charmed her *mother*. But Toni wasn't in the market for charm. Maybe she *was* playing it safe with Dan, but wasn't that how a relationship was supposed to make you feel? As if you really were safe. As if you really were with someone you could trust...

Just then Jackie and Hollan broke apart and came toward the table. Something was wrong, though. Only seconds ago the two of them had been lost in each other's arms, but now Jackie held herself stiffly, her expression one of hurt and outrage. As she reached the table, she ignored Kyle, staring only at Toni instead.

"Hollan Nash," she announced, her voice rigid, "is the stupidest human being I have ever known. And I never want to see him again!"

THE CABLE CAR RATTLED its way up the hill with a festive air on this sunny autumn day—Saturday-morning passengers spilling out the sides, the gripman cracking jokes as he slammed back the levers and clanged the bell.

"Everybody's in such a damn good mood," Hollan grumbled as he and Kyle clung to one of the poles of the cable car. Hollan had been grumbling all morning about one thing or another, but Kyle wasn't really listening to his friend. He gazed down the steep incline toward the bay. After ten years in San Francisco, he still enjoyed the hills of the city. He'd grown up on the flat prairie lands of west Texas, so he had a deep appreciation of hills. In fact, he didn't have many complaints about San Francisco—his adopted city wasn't responsible for the restlessness he'd been experiencing lately. The cause went a whole lot deeper than mere geography.

At the top of the hill, he swung off the cable car, Hollan coming behind.

"I still don't get it," Hollan said. "Why are we out traveling around with no place to go?"

"I'm the one wandering aimlessly," Kyle said. "You just came along so you could complain about your fiancée."

"She's driving me crazy," Hollan said.

No surprise there. From what Kyle could tell, Jackie Shaw had been driving Hollan crazy for the entire two months they'd been engaged. It seemed Jackie expected a lot in a man. It seemed Hollan was constantly in danger of falling short. Then again, Hollan expected a lot in a woman. It made for a volatile combination.

Kyle glanced toward the Bay Bridge. All down the hill, the high-rises on either side cast shadows over the street. "Too many damn office buildings," he muttered.

"Hey, don't knock 'em. It's how we make our living, remember?"

Kyle started walking and Hollan had to hurry to catch up.

"This aimless-wandering thing...you've been doing it a lot these past few weeks."

"Let's just say I'm thinking," Kyle said. "Thinking about what the hell I'm doing with my life."

"Rich and successful isn't enough anymore?" Hollan asked sarcastically.

"Maybe it was never enough. Maybe we're too successful, Hollan, and that's made us forget why we started out in this damn business."

"So do what I did," Hollan said. "Find the right woman."

"You just said she's driving you crazy," Kyle said. "Not to mention that last night she announced she never wanted to see you again."

"Yeah, that," Hollan said gloomily. "She'll come around. I mean, what did I do that was so bad? I was just trying to help. All I told her was that she should buy a car, and I should help her pick it out. She takes cabs everywhere. What kind of way is that to live?"

Kyle had already had a blow-by-blow description of last night's lovers' tiff. No sense in encouraging Hollan any further. Kyle stuffed his hands into the pockets of his jeans and walked on.

Hollan kept in step. "Tell me—what's so bad about wanting her to have her own transportation? I'm thinking about her welfare. It'd be a heck of a lot more convenient for her. And less dangerous, too—I'd make sure she got the safest model out there. Why should she put her life into the hands of a bunch of cabdrivers? I tried explaining all this to her, believe me I did, but then she said I only wanted her to have a car so I could keep her away from *my* car. Does that make any sense?"

"Considering that you treat your car like a shrine...yeah, I'd say it makes sense."

"Okay, so I don't want just anyone driving it. Does getting married mean I have to lose *everything* that's mine?"

"Your future wife's not supposed to be 'just anyone,'" Kyle said.

"She ate chocolate-covered cherries in my car—just the other day. We were on our way to...somewhere, I forget. But she started popping them right out of the box and into her mouth. You know what happens when somebody eats chocolate-covered cherries in your car?"

They'd already discussed the chocolate-covered-cherry incident. Kyle kept walking, kept trying to outpace the restlessness inside him.

"You never told me what you thought of the sister," Hollan said.

Antonia Shaw...Toni. She wasn't as flamboyant as Jackie, but that was what made her intriguing. Her beauty was more subtle, more alluring. Dark blond hair framing her face, eyes a shimmering blue-green. Last night she'd had her defenses up, that much was certain. It made him wonder what she'd be like if her guard ever came down.

Idle speculation. "The lady's spoken for," Kyle said. "She made sure I knew it."

"That's not what Jackie says," Hollan said. "According to Jackie, the sister's available in a big way...ripe for the picking. The guy she's seeing could bore the feathers off a chicken."

Kyle had liked being around Toni Shaw last night—liked it a lot, in fact. But when it came down to it...maybe *he* was the unavailable one.

After his latest disaster of a relationship, there definitely wasn't anyone in his life. And he didn't see himself being with a woman for quite some time to come. Not while this restlessness, this discontent, had hold of him. It was making him ask a lot of uncomfortable questions. Until he had the answers...no, there wouldn't be a woman in his life.

He and Hollan kept walking, the bustle of the city surrounding them. Other people hurried past as if they knew exactly where they were headed. Kyle seemed to be the only one who felt aimless at the moment.

"She's driving me crazy," Hollan repeated mournfully.

"If it's that bad," Kyle said, "have you ever considered...maybe you and Jackie aren't meant to be."

"You don't get it," said Hollan. "All my life, whenever I've met a girl, no matter who she was, somebody better always came along. But with Jackie it's not like that. She's the best, Kyle. No matter how much she drives me crazy, she's the best I'm ever going to get. It scares the hell out of me. Have you ever felt that way about anyone?"

Kyle thought it over. "No," he said. "Can't say I have."

Hollan gave him a look bordering on pity. The restlessness inside Kyle was joined by a peculiar emptiness. No woman in his life—and his career no longer made him happy. It had gotten too big, the small satisfactions vanished. He'd never realized how important those small satisfactions were until they were gone. But where did he go from here? What direction did he take without turning his back on all he and Hollan had accomplished together?

He didn't have the answers. All he had were questions.

## CHAPTER TWO

THE STACK OF FILES on Toni's desk seemed to be growing by the hour. She knew her boss wouldn't be happy about that. "Move 'em on through," he liked to say. He also liked to say, "We wouldn't want anyone to accuse *us* of jamming up the legal system."

Now Toni pulled the top file off the stack and opened it. Twenty-two-year-old white-collar male, accused of assaulting his ex-girlfriend. Another case that wouldn't make it to court, a plea bargain already in the works. The guy was guilty, no doubt about it, but he'd get away with a reduced charge, a fine, a few months' probation. That was the way it invariably happened in this office…crimes reduced, whittled down, made to seem less terrible than they actually were. All so the legal system wouldn't get jammed up, all so public defenders like Toni could keep moving their cases through.

"Damn," she said. She slapped the file closed and threw the thing across the room, angling it like a Frisbee. It landed at the feet of the man who'd just walked through her door…Kyle Brennan. He picked it up, tucked in the few sheets of paper that had come loose and placed it back on her desk. Then he smiled at her.

"Bad day?" he asked.

It had been exactly a week since she'd met Kyle at the restaurant in San Francisco. Frankly, she'd never expected to see him again. He was, after all, the best friend of Hollan Nash the Third. And Jackie had stated innumerable times during the week that she was absolutely, one hundred percent through with Hollan.

Unfortunately, that didn't change the fact that Hollan's best friend was still one of the most attractive men Toni had ever seen. His russet hair was a little untidy this evening, which only added to his appeal. He wore a charcoal suit and a burgundy tie...more appeal.

"Are you ready?" he said now.

"I'm ready to go home, if that's what you mean," she told him. "But what brings you to Heritage? This city is hardly on the tourist maps."

Heritage City was somewhat south and inland from San Francisco. However, the distance was more than a matter of miles. It was not quite small enough to be quaint, not quite large enough to be enterprising. It was, simply, Toni's hometown, the place she'd come back to after law school, the place she could never quite seem to get out of her system.

Kyle settled on a corner of her desk. His proximity

was both unsettling and enticing, bringing just the slightest whiff of cologne. A masculine, foresty scent.

Toni reshuffled her files. "Why *are* you here, Kyle?" she asked.

"Something tells me you don't know about our date tonight. Okay, it's not technically a date…call it a foursome. You, me, Jackie and Hollan, all spending a night on the town."

Toni stared at him. "You're joking. Hollan and Jackie broke up last Friday. This time I know I have the inside information—"

"Not the latest, apparently. They made up this morning. And Jackie's the one who asked me to pick you up here. She acted like you knew all about it."

Exasperation with her sister definitely had the upper hand again. Toni pushed back her chair and stood. "She didn't say a thing to me. Except for last night, when she called me and told me in excruciating detail how glad she was to be rid of Hollan. She's going to drive me crazy."

"Funny—that's exactly what Hollan says."

Kyle didn't seem perturbed by any of this. Instead, he appeared to be having a good time. He'd appropriated that corner of her desk as if prepared to stay.

"Listen, Kyle, I'm sorry you had to come all the way out here. Jackie had no business setting something up without consulting me. I'll talk to her and make sure it doesn't happen again. Meanwhile—"

"I know you don't have any plans for tonight," he said.

"What on earth makes you think that?"

He grinned. "It's Friday, remember? Dan's basketball night."

Toni wished heartily she'd never told Kyle anything about her personal life. "Just because...just because I'm not spending the evening with Dan doesn't mean I'm free."

"So what are your plans?"

Toni folded her arms. "I intend to go home and have a very pleasant meal by myself. And then I'm going to read a novel I've been wanting to start for ages."

Kyle got a confident look. "A novel and a meal...alone. You're right—I can't compete with that. Guess I'll have to send the limo back."

"Limo?" Toni went to the window and peered outside. Indeed, a sleek white limousine was parked at the curb. "I don't believe it," she said. "Are you telling me you came all the way out here from San Francisco in that thing? This is how you travel?"

"Tonight, it is. Limo and all the trimmings supplied courtesy of the awards committee."

She turned back to him. "Maybe you could stop being so mysterious. Maybe *somebody* could tell me what the heck's going on—"

"Hollan and I won an award for a building we de-

signed. I tried to talk myself out of the banquet tonight, but it was a no go. It means too much to Hollan—the guy's my friend, so what can I do? But I did
draw the line at a tuxedo."

Toni considered him. "You don't seem too thrilled
about the honor."

Now he stood and paced her small office. The humor no longer glinted in his eyes. "I'll tell you something about awards, Toni. They're usually somebody
else's idea about what's good, what's worthwhile. If
they don't match the way you feel, they don't mean a
whole lot."

"But if you and Hollan designed a building that
caught this much attention, it has to count for something."

"The design was adequate. It got the job done—
maybe even got it done well. That doesn't mean it's
a work of art, Toni, or that it should get any more
attention than it deserves."

"You want to make works of art?" she murmured.

"Lord, that would make me sound pompous,
wouldn't it? But no...I don't know what I want right
now. That's the problem." This time a look of frustration crossed his face. Toni couldn't help being intrigued by this glimpse into Kyle's life. He appeared
to be a man who had everything—looks, way too
much charm, an award-winning career. Yet something

was apparently missing, and he didn't even know what it was. Talk about a puzzle in need of solving...

He smiled wryly. "Whether we deserve it or not, they're throwing us a bash tonight. So what do you say?"

She glanced out the window again. "Limos aren't usually my style. That's more Jackie's type of thing."

"Funny, that's exactly what I was thinking."

She studied him. "Kyle, I know you came all the way out here because Jackie talked you into it, but—"

"Do you think your sister could talk me into anything I didn't want to do? Maybe I came out here for another reason."

She wished he wouldn't look at her that way. She couldn't concentrate as well as she'd like. "I'll tell you why you didn't mind coming out to see me," she said. "The fact that I'm unavailable means you can flirt outrageously with me—yet I'm no real threat to your bachelor lifestyle. Perfect combination."

He gave her that smile. "If Dan was smart, he'd schedule Friday nights for you."

"Saturdays and Wednesdays are more than sufficient—" She stopped herself, but not soon enough. "For crying out loud, I'll go to the banquet with you, Kyle. But it's *not* a date."

He nodded solemnly. "Definitely not. You're unavailable, and I have that bachelor lifestyle to protect."

The man was impossible. He was also irresistible.

He made her feel the way she did whenever she indulged in something wickedly delicious like a choco-
late-fudge sundae. She'd rationalize that the splurge
was acceptable because she didn't plan to do it again
for a long time to come. And that was what she was
doing now—rationalizing that an evening with Kyle
was acceptable because she didn't plan to do it ever
again.

She wondered briefly what Dan would think if he
knew she was going out with another man. But she
knew the likely answer. He wouldn't give it much
thought at all. He'd be too involved in his basketball
game.

She picked up her briefcase and headed out the
door. "We'll have to stop by my place so I can
change," she said.

Only a few moments later she and Kyle were settled
in the back seat of the limo, riding smoothly through
town. Kyle picked up what appeared to be a half-
finished conversation with the driver. It seemed he already knew the driver's name was Louis, and that
Louis was working on a degree in marketing while
moonlighting as a chauffeur. Kyle Brennan clearly did
not put on airs. Toni couldn't help being impressed by
that. She was also impressed by the way Kyle naturally opened the conversation to let her participate.
Considerate as well as devastatingly handsome...

Toni reminded herself not to overdo the catalog of

Kyle's good points. After tonight, she really didn't intend to see much of him again.

When they arrived at her apartment complex, Kyle escorted her up to the second floor. "You might as well come in," she said as she turned the key in the lock. "I won't be long." She felt self-conscious, though, as she led the way inside.

Everyone in her family believed her decor was too plain, too spare. But Toni loved clean, uncluttered lines, the feeling of spaciousness. She'd outfitted her living room with only a few choice pieces of furniture—a butternut chest that doubled as coffee table, a ladder-back rocking chair, a settee covered in faded needlework. A couple of oversize cushions on the floor offered extra seating. Toni had allowed exuberance on the walls, however, juxtaposing prints of nineteenth-century rural scenes with 1940s movie posters and a pegboard that displayed her collection of straw hats.

Kyle looked around carefully, as if noting every detail. He didn't speak at first, and Toni felt oddly suspenseful. But then he made his pronouncement.

"Nice," he said. "Very nice."

Toni was inordinately pleased. She suspected that he wouldn't have said it unless he was being sincere. Nonplussed by her overreaction to his compliment, she asked him to make himself comfortable, and disappeared into her bedroom and shut the door behind her.

Now she had to confront a different problem: what

to wear that would do justice to the limousine. She rifled through her closet, dissatisfied with everything she saw. It struck her that lately she'd let her wardrobe go too far in the lawyerly direction—uninspired jackets and skirts, tailored blouses, low-heeled pumps. She was starting to get a little desperate, when she finally decided on a mix that might just pass the test. She paired a short, narrow black skirt—one of her more frivolous purchases—with a white silk blouse. To avoid severity, she topped the outfit with a brightly embroidered vest, a favorite item of clothing she'd been toting around since her undergraduate days. Sheer dark hose, her one pair of shoes that could genuinely be called heels...well, she would just have to make do. There wasn't time for anything else. She tried to tame her hair with a brush, did something with lip gloss, dabbed on perfume, and then reminded herself this wasn't a date. She went out to Kyle.

His gaze traveled over her, slow and appreciative. He didn't say anything for a moment, but at last he spoke. "Your sister couldn't hold a candle to you," he said quietly.

She flushed. It was as if Kyle had seen inside her, had known her secret belief that she would never be as dazzling as her sister. She turned away from him.

"You're beautiful, Toni."

It seemed she had no choice but to look into his eyes. And the conviction came to her all over again—

he wouldn't have said it unless he meant it. This time it took more of an effort to glance away. Being alone with him suddenly felt too intimate.

"I'm ready, Kyle. Let's go collect your award."

SOME HOURS LATER, Toni was reminded yet again that her sister did not travel light. Lipstick, lip pencil, mascara, eyeshadow, eyeliner, eyebrow pencil, eyelash curler, face powder, blush, concealer. Jackie carried these with her at all times for what she called her "touch-ups." She insisted that in her line of work she couldn't afford not to look her best at any given moment. Jackie was a news anchor for an up-and-coming cable station in San Francisco—which meant that, admittedly, she was on constant public display.

Now Jackie leaned toward the mirror, carefully outlining her lips. She and Toni were in the ladies' room of San Francisco's Belgrave Hotel, occupying the lull between the banquet dinner and the awards ceremony. Jackie had already "touched up" just about every perfect detail of her appearance. Toni, in contrast, had simply done another pass with the lip gloss.

"Jackie," she said, "enough. I've been trying to catch a word with you all evening, and you keep finding excuses not to talk."

"What could we possibly talk about, except that we're having a wonderful time—"

"I can think of lots of things," Toni said. "Such

as why you didn't tell me about our little get-together tonight. And, for that matter, why you didn't let me know for two whole months that you were engaged. You still haven't owned up on that one.''

"Shh." Jackie looked concerned. "Keep your voice down," she said in a whisper. "I think we're the only ones in here, but you'd better go check the stalls just in case."

"For goodness' sake—"

"Toni, people eavesdrop on celebrities all the time, trying to get some snippet of news. Let's not make it easy for them."

Toni rolled her eyes. She couldn't dispute the fact that her sister *was* something of a minor celebrity—people recognized her on the street and waved to her whenever she passed by—but Jackie overdramatized everything.

"Jackie, I draw the line—I am not going to check the stalls."

"I'll do it then." Jackie crouched and started peering under the doors.

"You know," Toni said, "someone could be standing on one of the toilet seats. I've seen it in the movies."

"Very funny." Jackie straightened and came back to the mirror. "Okay, the coast is clear...you want to talk—let's talk. If I'd told you about the banquet beforehand, you wouldn't have come."

"What makes you think that?" Toni asked.

"*Would* you have come?"

"Heavens, no," Toni said. "I would have suspected you of trying to set me up with Kyle Brennan."

"He's a whole lot more exciting than Drippy Dan. Of course, *toast* is a whole lot more exciting than Dan. I can't imagine what you see in him. Okay, so there's no chance he'll break your heart the way Greg did, but still—"

"We're talking about you," Toni said firmly. "All week you've been calling me and telling me how rotten Hollan is, how selfish, and now suddenly the two of you are enthralled with each other again. Which is fine, but I still don't see why you can't let me in on these developments—"

"I'll tell you why." Jackie suddenly sounded passionate. She turned from her reflection and gazed at Toni. "Sometimes I get tired of feeling like such...such a *fool* around you, Toni. I tell you things, and you listen, but it's like the entire time you're thinking how *pathetic* I am. I can hear it in your voice. You think all I do is get involved with losers." Jackie took a deep breath and turned back to the mirror. She picked up one of her makeup brushes and applied blush to cheeks that already looked exactly the right shade of rosy. "Maybe a lot of them *have* been losers," she said. "I'd be the first to admit it. But Hollan's different. He's special. He's not like any man

I've ever known! So that's why I waited so long to tell you about the engagement. I knew you'd think, oh here she goes again, one more jerk, one more stupid decision. And I couldn't *bear* to have you think that…not about me and Hollan.''

"If you say Hollan is special, I believe you."

"You patronize me, that's what you do. I mean, it would have been too humiliating to call you today and tell you that I'd made up with Hollan. You would have thought I was being my usual erratic, illogical *self.* Admit it.''

Toni considered her sister's outburst. "Jackie, I try to keep an open mind. But the point is, you don't have to try for these dramatic surprises. Like springing the news of your engagement, or having Kyle Brennan show up in a limo. You act like all the drama will make what you do seem more justified…but it's not necessary. Hey, I'm your sister."

Jackie started tucking her supplies back into her purse. "All I want," she said, "is a little moral support from you. Is that so much to ask? For the first time in my life—the very first—I've found a man I can't afford to lose. Even when I'm mad as hell, and even when I think I don't ever want to see him again…I know I'll die if I lose him. It scares me, Toni…" She turned from the mirror. "How do I look?" she asked.

It amazed Toni that her sister could be so gorgeous, yet constantly need reassurance of this very fact.

"You're stunning, as usual," Toni said.

"Now let's get out there so we don't miss the awards ceremony," Jackie said. "Hollan's counting on me to share this recognition with him. He deserves all the awards in the world." She gave a misty-eyed smile. No one would ever guess that last night she'd been cursing the very name of Hollan Nash the Third.

They returned to the ballroom, and Toni slid into her chair beside Kyle at the head table. The banquet itself had been superb: oysters on the half shell, baby greens in lemon dressing, roast salmon with mushrooms, saffron rice—each dish light and delicate, tantalizing the palate while leaving room for the next course. By now, dessert had appeared, a compote of pineapple and tangerine. Kyle, however, didn't seem in the mood for any more delicacies.

"Wish they'd just get this thing over with," he muttered. Hollan, meanwhile, was glancing discreetly through note cards for his speech. The host for the evening, president of a national architectural society, finally stood and gave his introduction. Slides came up on a screen, showing the building Kyle and Hollan had designed. Toni could see why it had won an award. Fashioned of green stone the color of malachite, it seemed to be all windows and light. Paved courtyards flowed from the base, lending a sense that inside and outside space mingled. It was not a building where anyone would feel stifled or closed in; it had just the type of airiness that appealed to Toni. It had been constructed in Seattle—she hadn't realized that Kyle's and Hollan's talents were recognized so far afield.

She glanced at Kyle, and saw that he didn't seem impressed by the slides. He had a disgruntled look. When the podium was turned over to him, he gave possibly the shortest acceptance speech in history, a courteous but restrained "Thank you very much."

Then Hollan stepped up with his note cards, seemingly happy to take over where his partner had left off. It struck Toni that Jackie shared the same characteristic: a need to be in the spotlight, to occupy the center of attention. When finally all speechifying was done, and the elegant crystal award delivered, Jackie stood beside Hollan and received the congratulations of well-wishers as if she had somehow won an award, too. Certainly both Jackie and Hollan appeared to be in their element.

Not so Kyle. "What do you say we get out of here?" he asked Toni abruptly. "Let's go someplace where there's real entertainment."

"Kyle, I don't think it's such a good idea."

"Don't think about it then," he said. "Just come with me."

Toni gazed at him, and knew her first impression

had been right—Kyle Brennan was not a predictable man. Dangerously sexy, far too handsome for his own good…yes. But predictable…no.

"Kyle—"

"Just say yes." And then, without giving her a chance to answer, he drew her away from the ballroom and out into the nighttime sparkle of San Francisco.

# CHAPTER THREE

THE LIMO DROPPED THEM at the Dragon Gate—the entryway to Chinatown. Then Kyle led Toni into a world of neon lights and pagoda roofs, a world of spices and silks and lotus flowers, shops tempting with everything from teakwood and jade to kites and ginger and ginseng. Toni knew Chinatown well, but tonight, in Kyle's company, it seemed to take on a more exotic and unfamiliar atmosphere. Together they wandered, jostling elbows with other passersby on the narrow, crowded streets. When they were tired of walking, they ended up at a small bar where a jazz pianist played and where they were served lychee wine.

Kyle leaned back in his chair and loosened his tie. "Now," he said, "isn't this better than some damn banquet?"

Toni shook her head. "You know, Kyle, it wouldn't be so bad to admit you deserved the award. I don't think it would compromise your integrity too much."

"Toni...I'm just trying to remember what made me excited about architecture in the first place."

She propped her elbows on the table. The bar was

dim and smoky and conducive to private chats. "Well, what *did* make you excited?"

He smiled a little. "I'm thinking about the time when I was about thirteen or fourteen. My dad had this habit of starting projects and never finishing them. He'd got a kit to build a playhouse for one of my sisters, and the thing looked like it was going to be under construction forever. Dad had even lost the instructions. Finally I started experimenting myself. I put that playhouse together with my own design."

Toni tried picturing Kyle at thirteen or fourteen. "I'll bet your sister was pretty happy with you."

"Not really. The cost overruns almost set her back three weeks' allowance."

Perhaps it wasn't a good idea to find out details about Kyle's boyhood—it meant getting closer to him. But Toni couldn't seem to help herself. "You mentioned sisters, as in plural."

"Three altogether." He gave a wry grimace. "My mother said someday I'd be glad for all the sisters. She insisted that having sisters would make me understand women when I grew up."

Toni sipped her wine. "Was your mother right?" she asked. "Do you understand women?"

She didn't expect a serious response, but he surprised her. "I understand, all right," he said grimly. "I understand that lately I've had a string of bad luck. Sharon couldn't talk about anything but herself. All

Katherine wanted to do was cling. And Jan...well, I caught Jan on the rebound." Now Kyle was the one who propped his elbows on the table. The piano played low in the background. "I finally informed Hollan I was calling a moratorium on relationships. He was the one who kept fixing me up with these women. I said enough's enough. I need a break. It's bad enough trying to figure out what to do about my career. No more blind dates, I told Hollan."

"I see," Toni said. "And then you thought he was trying to set you up with *me*...only I'm safe because I'm already involved with someone."

Even in the dimness of this place, she saw the humor come back into Kyle's eyes. "Just how safe are you, Antonia? Hollan says that according to Jackie, this guy you're dating isn't even a contender. And what did your mother tell me over the phone? Something about you choosing Dan Greene because he couldn't hurt you the way you've been hurt before."

"Stop," Toni said. "I don't want to talk about it."

Kyle's gaze was too intent, too discerning. "Hurt pretty bad, were you? Anyone who could give you that expression...that sad expression...he's not worth the time you're still wasting on him."

"I'm not wasting time on him," Toni said. She realized that she'd spoken sharply, and she struggled to recover herself. "He's out of my life," she said after a moment. "I haven't seen him in almost four months."

"So you're still measuring time by how long it's been since you've seen him. A bad place to be, Toni."

She stared down at her clenched hands on the tabletop. "Kyle, could we please change the subject?"

He gazed at her as if about to say something else— something she wouldn't want to hear—but then he leaned back in his chair again.

"Fair enough," he said. "Change of subject. You know all about me and the infamous playhouse—it's your turn now. What made you decide to become a lawyer?"

She unclenched her hands. "That's easy. It was in college. I was an English major—a freshman, still trying to get used to such a big campus. First day for my class in the modern political novel, and I got lost. I ended up in the wrong building, and found myself sitting in on a criminology lecture. What can I say? I was hooked after that. Never went back to English."

"So now you're a public defender."

"If you want to call it that," she muttered. "Forget the public part—I'm always plea-bargaining instead of going to trial. Forget the defender part—my clients are usually looking for the easiest way out, not looking to redeem their honor."

"If there's one thing I'm good at," Kyle said, "it's detecting a career crisis."

Toni sighed. This wasn't such a comfortable subject, after all. "I've had the job two years," she said. "And I keep asking myself—aren't I supposed to be helping people? Aren't I supposed to be making a difference somehow? Aren't I supposed to be practicing real law, instead of shuffling cases off my desk as fast as I can?"

Kyle didn't offer any reassuring answers.

"I'm starting to feel pretty useless," she went on. "I show up at work, I go through all the motions…ha, motion to dismiss, that's the main one. But you know the one concrete thing I'm doing? Building up vacation days, one after the other. By now I probably have enough time coming to me for the grand tour of Europe."

"Is that what you'd like?" Kyle asked.

"I'd rather feel like my work mattered somehow, but I wouldn't turn Europe down. Although, when it comes to vacations, there's one place closer to home I never get enough of. My dad and I have a piece of land up north a little ways—we inherited it from Grandpa Shaw." She smiled wistfully. "Funny old Grandpa Shaw. He was eighty-seven when he died, but that didn't make it any easier to lose him. He always had stories to tell me about when he was young. And he always had a way of making me feel special. The only one in the family who acted like I was his favorite." Maybe she'd revealed too much. Kyle was giving her a thoughtful look.

She hurried on. "Anyway, Grandpa left the land to my dad and me. Grandpa knew how much I loved to go up there with him. If only you could see it, Kyle. It's in a valley, but we have our own little piece of mountain, too. There's a vineyard nearby, and when everything turns red and gold in the fall, the way it's probably doing right now, I can't think of anyplace that makes me feel more peaceful.... Well, anyway," she said inadequately, "if I were going to take a vacation, I suppose that's where I'd go. But instead I just keep on showing up at work...shuffling more cases across my desk. Isn't it about time for a change?"

He still didn't have any answers for her. How could he? The man was going through a career crisis of his own.

"Kyle, I think we should get back to the banquet. Jackie and Hollan will wonder where we went off to."

"I doubt it. They've probably forgotten all about us."

Toni was pretty sure he was right. "Nonetheless...I just think you and I shouldn't do this type of thing anymore."

"What type of thing, Antonia?"

She wished he wouldn't say her name that way. Every time, it sent a warm little tingle down her spine.

"You know what I mean," she said. "Going off together, and having what *almost* amounts to a date."

"Almost...I think I like 'almost.'" He gave her a slow grin. The problem was, she liked "almost" too.

"Look, Kyle," she said, "you're Hollan's best friend, and I'm Jackie's sister...and that's as far as it goes. Neither one of us really wants anything more."

"Then why are we here together?" he said, and he gave her that smile again. And for a moment, just a moment, she asked herself that very same question. What *was* she doing here with the most handsome man she'd ever met?

MONDAY MORNING, Kyle found himself paying a visit to the public defender's office in Heritage City. As he approached Toni's cubbyhole toward the back of the building, he heard the murmur of her voice.

"Dan, I just thought we could do something different this time. I don't know, hit the movies on *Monday* night for once. Why does it always have to be Wednesday? No...no, I am not being snide. I happen to love routines I can set my watch by...no, that wasn't snide, either...where's your sense of humor? Yes, I'm aware that you do have one..."

Kyle thought maybe he should let his presence be known. He stepped into the room.

Toni straightened. She'd been sitting with her feet up on the desk—and now her feet came down with a thump. "Dan…I'll have to call you back. Yes, I do realize your staff meeting starts exactly at ten o'clock, not a minute later…yes, I was being snide that time. Goodbye, Dan." She hung up, then gave Kyle a belligerent look.

"Lately Dan's been a wee bit sensitive about what I call his routines," she said. "He seems to think I'm being critical."

"Hmm…the guy's a stick-in-the-mud, and he knows it."

Toni frowned. "Kyle, what on earth are you doing here again?"

He didn't think it was the right time to answer that, so he just stood there gazing at her. She looked very pretty of a Monday morning. She was wearing a red scarf in her hair, and businesslike blouse and slacks that couldn't quite disguise her curves.

"Kyle, why *are* you here? I thought we agreed we weren't going to see each other outside the confines of…you know, our relationship with Jackie and Hollan."

"I don't remember agreeing to that," he said.

"We were at that bar in Chinatown on Friday night, and I distinctly remember that I told you—" She stopped herself, and gave him an aggravated look. "I should know better, shouldn't I?"

"Yes," he said, "you should."

"Kyle...I really would like to know why you're here."

He could tell she wouldn't be easily convinced, but he went ahead. "Item one, you have excessive vacation days built up. Item two, you never get a chance to go visit that land of your grandpa's. Item three, I happen to have a free day myself. Item four...my car's waiting at the curb."

"You're joking," she said. "You can't just come down here on the spur of the moment, and take me away from...from—"

"Another phone call to reliable old Dan?" he suggested.

She tried to give him a strict look. Unfortunately, her sexy red scarf ruined the effect. "Kyle," she said, "why are you doing this?"

He didn't have a good answer for that one. He knew, deep down, that it wasn't the smartest idea in the world to have come here. He should have resisted the urge to see her.

"Look, Toni," he said, "all I know is that it's a beautiful day out there, and neither one of us should waste it being stuck in an office. We both need to get away from the stuff that's bothering us. Maybe we both need some perspective...and maybe we'll find it up north. Besides, it's a convertible...with a picnic basket in the back."

She didn't say anything for a long moment. Several

emotions seemed to do battle across her lovely, expressive face. And then, at last, she gave a small shrug. "A convertible... I'll go tell my boss I'm taking the rest of the day off." She took the navy jacket that had been draped over the back of her chair, and slipped it on. Instantly she looked a whole lot more like a lawyer. Straightening her collar and smoothing her lapels, she went out of the office. Kyle watched her walk down the hall.

It didn't take Toni long to come marching back again. "It's all set. Let's do it. Let's get out of here before I come to my senses." She picked up her cellular phone and began putting it inside her briefcase.

"You won't need that," he said. "No phones today. And no briefcase."

She negotiated. "I'll give in on the phone, but the briefcase...can't leave that behind. It doubles as my purse." She buckled the straps and swung the case by her side. She looked more like a lawyer than ever.

But that red scarf held out hope to Kyle.

# CHAPTER FOUR

TONI WAS NO CONNOISSEUR of automobiles, but as she sat beside Kyle in his silver convertible, she could tell what a fine vehicle it was. It had a canvas top, folded back neatly, so that Toni felt as if the vivid blue sky above had been invited right into the car. The engine hummed along eagerly all the way from Heritage City to San Francisco and then across the Golden Gate Bridge to points north.

"Good taste," Toni murmured at last. "That's what you have, Kyle. I guess I knew that from the first time I saw you."

He glanced at her, his hands resting casually, expertly on the wheel. "Good taste...yes, I like to think so." His eyes lingered on her just a bit before he concentrated on the road again.

"I'm referring to the car," she said dryly. "But I'm sure you already knew that."

"I'd be glad to talk to you in great, annoying detail about this baby. Or maybe I'll just tell you she has a lot of excitement under the pedal."

Excitement... Toni had no doubt there was always

excitement somewhere in Kyle Brennan's life. She knew she should berate herself for giving in to him today. On the other hand, she couldn't help settling back and enjoying the scenery. This was wine country, the scent of newly harvested grapes on the air. The autumn vineyards spread their gold and crimson over the valley floor and up the hillsides.

As Kyle drove on, Toni could feel herself relax more and more, the thread of tension inside her slowly beginning to unwind. Neither she nor Kyle spoke as the miles flowed under the wheels. For now, conversation did not seem necessary. Toni sensed that Kyle appreciated the landscape as much as she did.

He downshifted as they came into a small, sun-drenched town. Shops clustered around the central plaza, along with a rakish, weather-beaten saloon, a remnant of California's gold rush days. Here and there low adobe houses had been layered over with Victorian gingerbread, hinting at the mix of cultures that had always pleased Toni. But still they had not reached *her* territory. She directed Kyle onto a narrow winding road, and the landmarks most special to her began to appear.

"That barn over there," she said, "the one that looks like it's about to tumble down—Grandpa used to play there as a kid with his best friend. And the grove up ahead, that's where Grandpa first kissed my grandmother. They were only teenagers when they fell in love..." Toni stopped herself. "Sorry," she said. "Grandpa was full of stories, and they all come flooding back to me whenever I'm up here."

"You're lucky to have that kind of heritage," Kyle said.

"Yes, well...the thing is, for everyone else in my family, Grandpa's ramblings were just something to be tolerated."

"But for you they were something to be remembered."

"Yes," Toni murmured. "That's it exactly. I could see Grandpa getting old. And I could see that someone had to pay attention to his stories, or they'd be lost."

"Your grandpa was lucky, too," Kyle said.

Toni gazed out the windshield. She hadn't spoken to anyone about her grandfather in a very long while. But Kyle seemed to understand so naturally...so well.

The road curved through fields and apple orchards. Weathered cottages nestled among grape arbors, now and then an old windmill turned lazily in the breeze. And here, at last, was Toni's land—a meadow that stretched out beyond the neighboring vineyard, and was sheltered by the oak-forested hillside rising above. Kyle pulled off the road onto a rutted track. Then he came to a stop, the silver convertible surrounded by wildflowers.

Toni slipped out of the car, and Kyle joined her. Together they walked across the meadow.

"Grandpa grew up on a dairy farm not far from here," Toni said. "His parents ended up selling it and moving to the city, but Grandpa himself held on to this one patch of land. He said he had to have something to remind him that he was a farm boy at heart."

"It was a good decision," Kyle said. He glanced around thoughtfully, then walked on with Toni until they reached the first gentle rise of the hill.

"Come on," said Toni. "I know the perfect spot. I appropriated it when I was about ten years old." She climbed a short distance up the hill, making her way among the trees. But then the ground cleared, allowing a generous knoll that overlooked the valley. Toni sat down in the long grass, drawing up her knees and wrapping her arms around them. Kyle sat beside her.

"I used to stay here for hours when I was a kid," she murmured. "I pretended that everything I saw was my domain...the fields and the vineyards and the orchards. My own special kingdom."

Kyle leaned back, propping himself on one elbow. "I'm glad you brought me here," he said.

She gave him a bemused glance. "I think it's the other way around. You brought *me*. You practically kidnapped me from my office."

"So...aren't you glad I did it?"

"Yes," she admitted. "I am. I wish I could come out here more often. When I was younger, I even wished I could have a house out here. It's a crazy idea, of course.''

''Why crazy?'' he asked.

''My life is in Heritage. I can't just drop everything and hole up in the country.''

''Too bad,'' he said reflectively.

''It's a dream, that's all. My dream house...'' She gave a shrug.

After that, they passed another long while in companionable silence. The weather provided a perfect combination of cool breeze and warm sun. Toni slipped off her jacket. She treated the garment unceremoniously, bunching it up and placing it behind her head as a pillow. Reclining comfortably in the grass, she allowed her eyelids to drift downward. Toni was not given to morning naps—not in the least. Ever since law school, she'd developed a work ethic that scarcely allowed naps at any time. But right now she simply couldn't stop herself. She drowsed. It seemed to be something marvelously decadent and self-indulgent, dozing in the morning sun. Kyle would probably have no difficulty indulging, either.

It was the thought of Kyle Brennan that finally nudged Toni back to wakefulness. She turned her head bit by bit and snuck a look at him. Yes, just as she'd imagined. He, too, was stretched out comfortably, his arms linked behind his head, his eyes closed, the smallest smile playing at his lips. Toni's gaze traveled down the jeans-clad length of his legs, then back up to the cream-colored polo shirt he wore. Good taste, unquestionably.

When she glanced at his face again, she saw that he wasn't asleep, after all. His eyes were open, and he was studying her.

Toni sat up rather too abruptly. "I don't know what's gotten into us," she said. "We're just lounging around...doing nothing."

"Isn't that the idea?" Kyle asked.

"I don't know what the idea is," Toni grumbled. "Except you said something about us getting some perspective out here."

"Don't you have any yet?"

The only perspective she'd gotten so far was a good view of Kyle's well-formed physique. Now she took her jacket and tried to smooth it out. "I think we should head back," she said briskly.

"Hey, aren't you hungry?" he asked.

"Actually, yes, but—"

"I promised you a picnic, didn't I?"

She found herself gazing into his dark brown eyes. "I'd forgotten," she said.

"When someone offers you a picnic, well...that's something special. We're talking one of the truly great pleasures of life."

"Picnics," she said doubtfully.

"Antonia, when was the last time you had a picnic?"

Picnics sounded as decadent and indulgent as morning naps. "I can't exactly remember," she said. "They've never been a big part of my life."

Kyle shook his head. "Toni, I can tell your horizons need expanding. Wait right here." He stood and disappeared among the trees. A few moments later, Toni watched as he emerged onto the meadow and headed for the car. Kyle seemed very much at home in these surroundings.

A short while later, leaves rustled as he came back up the hill, appearing beside her once more. She inspected the basket he was holding. It was the old-fashioned type, big and sturdy, with a hinged lid.

"Tell me," she said skeptically, "you just happened to have this picnic basket lying around the house."

"Yeah, I did. It used to belong to my Aunt Eileen."

"Aunt Eileen..."

"Sure," said Kyle. "She still lives in Amarillo. When she heard I was moving to the wilds of California, she packed me off with a great picnic lunch. I never did get around to returning the basket."

"I don't believe a word you're saying."

"Aunt Eileen would be offended." He opened the lid of the basket and took out a gingham cloth, which he proceeded to spread on the grass.

"I'll admit, that looks like something an Aunt Eileen would provide."

"Told you." Next came a braided French bread, along with a bottle of wine.

Toni picked up the bottle and read the label. Fine California vintage, perhaps even produced at one of the wineries they'd passed today. "Is this what Aunt Eileen recommends?"

"Aunt Eileen's specialty is homemade pear juice. Gosh-awful stuff, but she *is* my aunt." Kyle produced a round of Gruyère cheese and a jar of dill pickles.

"Aunt Eileen of Amarillo," Toni mused. "You're telling me that you're a Texan?"

"The Panhandle. Only place in God's country a person should be from. That's what Aunt Eileen says, anyway."

Toni wondered if she'd imagined it—or had Kyle just now spoken with a hint of a drawl? She gave him a careful look. "I guess I can picture it," she said. "You on the wide-open plains...you probably had a horse, didn't you?"

"Yep. Filly name of Nutmeg. She was a good cow horse, but she's retired now. She pastures at my cousin's ranch."

Toni hadn't been mistaken, after all. Kyle had definitely done it again—that subtle drawl. An urbane California architect with a taste of Texas...a potent combination.

"Sounds like you have a close family," she said, "if Aunt Eileen is any indication."

"The Amarillo Brennans," he mused. "Close, all right. You should see the Saturday-night get-togethers. Brennans have a penchant for old Hollywood musicals. Come Saturday night, every Fred Astaire–Ginger Rogers video in the city is rented out."

Toni gave him a sharp look. "Now I know you're kidding."

"I'm completely serious," he said. "We grew up watching old musicals from the thirties and forties. Funny thing, though. None of us turned out to be dancers or singers. I chose architecture. One of my sisters is in medical school, and two are teachers. My mother's a physical therapist. Dad's an engineer. Aunt Eileen sells real estate. Not a single one of us can tap-dance or carry a tune."

Toni watched as Kyle produced two apples, a bag of potato chips, some chocolate-chip cookies, granola bars, another round of gourmet cheese, an avocado, a tomato and three walnut-cranberry bagels.

"I think," said Toni, "that Aunt Eileen would be proud."

Kyle grinned at her. "Now you've got the spirit."

It was delectable. They made pickle-avocado-cheese-and-tomato sandwiches; she never would have imagined the combination could be so delicious. Apples and wine, and the sun shining down...

Together they polished off a surprising number of chocolate-chip cookies. "Not another bite," Toni said at last. "Goodness, did you buy the jumbo size potato chips?"

"I didn't want to run out."

"No fear of that." A few more potato chips, one final cookie… "Now I really am done," Toni declared. She wondered if everything tasted so good because she was outdoors on a beautiful day, or because she was enjoying the company. Perhaps it was a little of both.

Another companionable silence stretched between them. Toni didn't know how many moments passed. Keeping track of time seemed unnecessary, just as words seemed unnecessary. It occurred to her that comfortable silence was not usually something she shared with a man. Certainly not with Dan. Maybe she hadn't even shared it with Greg…

"You have that look again," Kyle murmured. "That sad look."

Toni busied herself putting things back in the basket.

"This guy who hurt you," Kyle said. "You're still wasting time on him, aren't you?"

Good-looking *and* mind-reading skills, she thought. Toni took a deep breath. "I don't think about Greg very often. And when a random thought *does* occur to me…I banish it as soon as possible."

"So," Kyle said. "Greg is his name."

Toni clasped her hands together and stared down at them. "Oh, hell," she muttered. "Let's just get this out in the open and over with. You might as well know what happened. Greg asked me to marry him. I said yes. I thought everything was fine. But then...well, I guess you could say he got a classic case of cold feet. He started sleeping with another woman. And then he made damn sure I would find out about it. It's easy to leave little signs around, little details for the discovering. So I discovered them—and I broke it off. That turned out to be just what Greg wanted. A way out. He got it, all right." Toni realized she was clenching her hands. She had a habit of doing that whenever the subject of Greg came up. With an effort, she relaxed her muscles. "Anyway," she said, "that's the whole story, pathetic as it is."

Kyle didn't say anything. He just went on studying her in the thoughtful way he had, giving her the unsettling feeling that he saw far too much.

"We have to go, Kyle," she said at last.

"Not just yet." He stood and wandered along the grassy ridge. He stopped some distance from Toni, apparently lost in thought. She was glad to have a little time to collect herself. She finished packing up the basket. By the time she was done, she felt once more calm and in control.

Kyle walked back toward her. She'd already decided that if he tried to bring up her personal problems again, she'd change the subject. But when Kyle spoke, it seemed he had something different on his mind.

"I told you I wanted to get some perspective, Toni. Seems maybe I'm seeing things all too clearly." He paused, then, "You know how my life feels right now? Like the shell of a house. On the outside it looks like a home, but when you go up close...when you cup your hands on the glass and peer inside the windows, you don't see any furnishings, any people inside. It's just empty. So I'm asking the question you asked the other night—isn't it time for a change?" He sounded intense. He also sounded determined.

"I'm all for change," Toni said. "If something's not working out, you try a new tack. Why not?"

They gazed at each other, but at last Toni had to look away. She stood and picked up the picnic basket.

"We really do have to go, Kyle. We have to get back to real life."

He glanced out over the valley. "Don't you think this is more real than anything else you have?"

Toni gave a shrug. "This is a place for dreams. My ordinary, day-to-day life is back in Heritage City."

"Toni...maybe it's not such a good idea to settle for ordinary."

"I'm not settling," she said. "I'm just trying to have the best life I can." She went down the hill. Crossing the meadow, she returned the picnic basket to the car. Then she slid into the passenger seat. It took Kyle a little while to follow her. When finally he did get into the driver's seat, he seemed lost in thought again. Neither of them spoke as he started the engine and drove to the road. At the last minute, though, Toni turned her head around for one last view of Grandpa's land. *Her* land...

The convertible sped back the way they had come, taking each curve of the road with an effortless grace. Kyle rested one hand on the gearshift knob. Toni studied the strong shape of his fingers, and the appealing smattering of freckles on his skin. She found herself wishing that they could slow down, prolong this day after all.

A short time later the smooth ride suddenly turned thumpy. Kyle decelerated and pulled off to the side of the road. "Sounds to me like a flat tire."

"Sounds that way to me, too."

He climbed out and went to examine the left rear wheel. "Yep," he said. "She's flat, all right. Looks like we picked up a good-size nail." He didn't sound perturbed. In fact, that spice of a drawl was back.

Toni climbed out and watched as he pulled the spare from the trunk. Then he stopped.

"This beats everything," he said. "The spare's flat, too."

She came to examine the tire. "You can't be serious—"

"Afraid so."

She frowned. "Aren't you supposed to check the thing for air every now and then?"

He gave a rueful grin. "Probably. But with a car like this, you tend to forget ordinary, day-to-day details like checking the spare."

"Right," Toni muttered. "You just think about all that excitement under the pedal. Well...we'll have to call for help, that's all." She began reaching for her briefcase, only to remember that she hadn't brought her cell phone along. "We'll have to use your phone," she said. Then she saw regret flicker across his face. "Oh, don't tell me," she groaned. "You left yours behind, too?"

"Antonia, it just didn't seem like a day for phones."

He didn't appear particularly repentant, and Toni gave him a suspicious glance. "Kyle, you didn't *plan* this, did you?"

"Hey, maybe I wanted to steal you away, but sabotaging my own car is going a little too far—even for me."

She sighed. She believed him, of course. Kyle Brennan was not a man who would need to resort to subterfuge.

"You have to be at least a little concerned," she said. "Here we are...stuck. A flat tire, a flat spare, not a phone between us and not a house in sight."

He leaned against the car. "It all comes back to perspective," he said gravely. "Just a matter of how you look at things. Sure, we're stuck. But the surroundings are nice. We still have some food left. Come to think of it, nothing beats eating under the stars."

All Toni could do was stare at him. She remembered her own wish that the day could be prolonged. The wish had come true—and somehow she wasn't sorry.

She remembered something else, a piece of advice Grandpa had once given her. He'd said that you could always judge a man by the way he reacted in a crisis. Did he keep his head? Did he take charge of the circumstances, instead of the other way around? Grandpa had said those were the qualities to look for. Maybe this qualified as a crisis...a mini-crisis, anyway.

Just then an old truck came rattling down the road, then stopped beside Kyle and Toni. A man, woman and little boy were all piled into the front of the truck. The man poked his head out the window. "A flat tire, eh?" he said.

Toni actually regretted the interruption. She wished she and Kyle could still be alone together...she wanted to go on being stuck with him.

"Guess we do need some help," Kyle said. Was it possible he sounded reluctant, too? "Maybe you could give us a lift to the nearest pay phone."

Just then the little boy scrambled out of the truck

and came darting over to the convertible. He pulled himself up short at the last minute, shyness obviously overcoming his interest in the car.

"Hey there," Kyle said.

"Hello," the boy answered. He was probably nine or ten years old, with shaggy brown hair and a pair of too-big glasses perched on his nose.

Kyle nodded at the convertible. "Don't suppose you'd want to sit behind the wheel for a minute, see what she feels like."

The little boy's face lit up. Kyle opened the door for him, and he scooted into the driver's seat. Now the man climbed out of the truck. The convertible seemed to have caught his interest, too.

"Easy, Nathan," he told the boy, who was cranking away at the steering wheel. "This is not your car." Then he addressed Kyle. "How much horsepower you got here?"

"Two-eighty-five. She's a V-6." Kyle popped the hood, and the two of them leaned into the engine compartment.

The woman got out of the truck and came over to Toni. "My guys are car crazy," she said in mock despair. "Ernie's bad, but the son's even worse. I hope you weren't in a hurry."

Toni smiled. There was something appealing about the way the woman had spoken—affectionately laying claim to her family as "my guys."

"Nathan, you heard your father. Be gentle with that wheel."

Kyle poked his head out from under the hood. "He's okay. Looks like you have a future race-car driver on your hands."

"Don't I know it," said the woman. "Nathan...gently!"

It occurred to Toni that a lot of men would cringe at having a kid haul on the steering wheel of a prize convertible. Not Kyle. He just began explaining to Nathan how the headlights worked.

"Your boyfriend's nice," the woman informed Toni.

"He's not my boyfriend," Toni said.

"Oh...too bad."

Toni flushed. If Kyle had heard, he made no sign. Now he was demonstrating the intricacies of the six-speed gearbox to the boy.

After another short while, the convertible had been thoroughly inspected and appreciated, and Nathan had accepted some chocolate-chip cookies from the picnic basket. It was time to go.

"I hope you don't mind piling in the back," the woman said to Toni and Kyle. "We're kind of cramped as it is up front."

"No problem," Kyle said. He helped Toni and her briefcase—as well as the picnic basket—into the bed of the truck. Husband, wife and son climbed into the front, and off they all went, rumbling down the road. Kyle and Toni shared space with two large tubs of green apples.

Kyle turned his head and gazed at her. And then, without a word, he took her hand in his. The warmth of his touch seemed to envelop her. But she did not pull away. She allowed her hand to stay right where it was, tucked inside Kyle's, while the magic of the day surrounded them.

# CHAPTER FIVE

"TONI, HOW COULD YOU do it! Kyle's defected!"

Toni winced, and held the phone away from her ear for a second or two. Jackie got a little loud when she was upset.

"I don't have any idea what you're talking about," Toni said. "Start at the beginning, Jackie."

"Hollan's in a tizzy. I mean, he can't believe that Kyle would do it—walk out on their partnership! And it's all your fault, Toni. You're the one who convinced him."

Toni sighed. "Jackie, I didn't convince Kyle to do anything. And what do you mean, he's walked out on the partnership?"

"He quit. He left. *Adios...arrivederci... sayonara!* How else can I say it? Kyle told Hollan you took him on a picnic, and that's when he 'saw the light.' That's where he decided he was going to change his life. So you see, it *is* your fault."

Toni paced back and forth in her living room with the phone in her hand. She still couldn't believe what she was hearing. It was only yesterday that she and

Kyle had gone out to Grandpa's land. Kyle had expressed some discontent with his life, but he'd certainly said nothing about turning it upside down.

Jackie was already rushing on. "Hollan says he can't even think about wedding plans when his best friend has just up and walked out on the business. He says we might even have to postpone the nuptials. After we'd finally agreed on a date, and everything... Oh, Toni, why did you do this to me?" Jackie sounded on the verge of tears.

"Jackie," Toni said as patiently as possible, "Kyle is the type of man who makes up his own mind. Besides, this is between him and Hollan—"

"You have to talk to Kyle. You have to convince him to come back to the firm!"

Toni paced again, trailing the phone cord behind her. "Jackie, listen to me. Yesterday, after Kyle brought me home, I told him I couldn't see him anymore."

"Now, why on earth," said Jackie, "did you do that?"

Toni stood still, and thought about it. Somehow, being with Kyle had made everything seem like such a wonderful adventure. The picnic, and then bouncing along in that old truck... She'd almost been sorry when they'd finally gotten the tire fixed and Kyle had driven her home. But, once on her doorstep, she'd come back to reality. She'd realized that the last thing she needed was Kyle Brennan in her life.

"Toni," said Jackie. "Please don't tell me this has anything to do with Drippy Dan."

"Actually it's not fair to Dan for me to...go out and about with Kyle."

"Let me get this straight," Jackie said. "You're not even having *sex* with Dan, but you're acting like the guy has exclusive rights."

Toni winced. "Let's not discuss my sex life."

"What sex life?"

Toni wished heartily that she'd never discussed the matter with her sister. The truth was, Dan had been pressing to take their relationship to "the next level," as he called it. Toni wasn't ready for the next level. She'd made the mistake of confiding that to Jackie.

"I think we're off the subject," she told Jackie now.

"First you mess with Kyle's head, then you say you can't see him because of Dorky Dan. And meanwhile, Hollan's twisted in knots and he wants to *postpone*. Just do something to straighten this out, Toni. Please—do it for me!" And with that, Jackie dramatically cut the connection.

Toni sank into her rocker. She was still trying to take in the fact that Kyle had quit his partnership with Hollan. And to say that he'd done it because of *her*...that was the part she just couldn't accept. Maybe she did have a little straightening out to do. She got up and went to the hall cabinet, where she kept the San Francisco phone directories. Lugging them back to the rocker, she sat down again and started riffling through the residential listings.

There he was…Brennan, Kyle. She dialed the number. After a few rings, an answering machine clicked on. Kyle's voice told her he was not available, but she could leave a message. Toni hung up.

Next she went through the business listings. There it was…Nash and Brennan Architects. She dialed the number, only to be connected to his secretary.

"I'm sorry, Mr. Brennan is not available at this time," said the efficient voice on the other end. "No, Mr. Nash is not available, either."

Toni was really starting to be annoyed by that phrase—"not available." She glanced at her watch. It was after five, and there was no telling when or how she'd be able to reach Kyle.

"Please tell Mr. Brennan that Toni Shaw called."

"Oh, Ms. Shaw. Mr. Brennan left some time ago to keep his appointment with you. I'm surprised he's not already there."

Toni frowned. "I don't have an appointment with Kyle."

"Oh, but you do, Ms. Shaw," the woman said maddeningly. "Mr. Brennan asked me to look up the address for Mr. Charles Shaw in Heritage City. He said he was proceeding there directly, to speak with Mr.

Shaw and his wife." The woman paused. "So naturally, I assume you're Mr. Shaw's wife—"

"More like Mr. Shaw's daughter. Thank you. Goodbye." Toni hung up the phone and stared at it. What on earth was Kyle up to? Why did he have a so-called appointment with her parents, of all people?

"Only one way to find out," Toni muttered to herself. She grabbed her briefcase and headed out the door.

It was only a short distance to her parents' house. And, sure enough, when she arrived, she saw Kyle's convertible parked out front. Toni went up the walk and pushed open the front door. Even though both Toni and Jackie had moved out long ago, they were expected to treat their parents' house as their own. Marianne Shaw liked the fact that her daughters could "drop in" at any moment.

Inside the house, the usual homey clutter greeted Toni: Dad's collection of maps crowding the walls, a stack of Mom's books and magazines piled haphazardly on the hall table, Dad's briefcase tossed willynilly in a corner, Mom's golf clubs propped beside a stand-up lamp.

Animated voices came from the living room. As she stepped into the room, the tableau that greeted her was remarkably cozy: her pleasantly balding father with his feet up in the recliner, her pretty, blond-haired mother in the armchair opposite—and Kyle Brennan on the sofa, holding the family dachshund, Genevieve.

It appeared that Toni had interrupted quite a lively conversation. Her mother turned to her, breaking out in a smile.

"Darling, isn't it wonderful?" she asked Toni. "Mr. Brennan is going to design a house for you!"

"Excuse me?" Toni said, as politely as possible under the circumstances.

"You remember our discussion, Toni?" Kyle asked genially. "Yesterday you told me you'd like a house on your grandfather's land. A dream house, I believe you called it."

"It wasn't a discussion. It was wishful thinking. A remark I made in passing—" She stopped and gave him a hard look. There was something different about him tonight. Underneath the humor, the relaxed attitude, she sensed a new intensity. It showed in his eyes, in the way he gazed back at her.

"A house—" she began.

"A house," Marianne said. "It really is a wonderful idea. Toni has lived in apartments far too long. She needs a house."

Toni sat down in the armchair across from her mother's. She took a deep breath. "Would someone please tell me what the heck is going on?" she asked, once again making every effort at politeness.

"As Mr. Brennan told you—we're talking about a

house on your grandpa's land," said her father. "It's something we've discussed before, you know—maybe putting a cabin up there. But what Mr. Brennan has in mind—a real house—that makes a lot more sense. It's worth considering."

Kyle didn't say anything. He just sat there on the sofa with the dog in his lap, looking perfectly at home.

Toni was afraid that if she spoke she wouldn't be so polite after all. She took another deep breath. When she felt she could trust herself, she addressed Kyle.

"Mr. Brennan," she said acidly, "there's a slight problem with your plan. I'm not in the market for a house. Besides, your firm—which I believe you've just quit—builds office towers."

"Yes, dear," said Toni's mother. "Mr. Brennan has already told us all about that. He doesn't want to design office buildings anymore. He wants to design houses. And he feels that your house would be the perfect place to start."

"Whoa! Back up a little," Toni said. "Kyle, you can't just quit your partnership and then come over here and start talking about a *house*. Especially without consulting me first."

"Just tossing the idea around," Kyle said amenably.

"It's worth consideration," Toni's father said. "Of course, it's a big decision, and we'll have to give it some serious thought before we make up our minds, but Mr. Brennan understands that. He's a business-man.''

"Mr. Brennan also has excellent credentials," Toni's mother put in.

Toni stared at Kyle. "What did you do—bring along your résumé?"

"In my line of work, it's more a portfolio." He grinned at her.

Toni stood, walked over to Kyle and plucked the dog away from him. Then she sat down again, cradling Genevieve. "A house on Grandpa's land isn't practical right now," she said. "My life is centered here in Heritage. It's not like I could move up north."

"So think about the future," said her mother. "You may decide to sell the land at some point, and a house will raise the value."

"I'd never sell Grandpa's land," Toni said emphatically.

"Okay, scratch that," said her mother, irrepressible as ever. "But think about this. The land clearly means a lot to you—and, with a house, you could spend weekends up there. Wouldn't that be nice."

Toni gave her mother a suspicious look. Dad was treating this like a business proposition to be taken under consideration. Mom, however, was pushing the idea wholesale. Why?

Now Marianne stood and went toward the kitchen. "Mr. Brennan is staying for dinner, Toni."

"Of course," Toni said under her breath.

"What was that?"

"Nothing, Mom."

"You'll stay, too, dear. I've made a mushroom loaf I think you'll enjoy."

Toni's dad and Kyle had already started another conversation. The two of them seemed to be getting along just great. Toni wanted to holler. Instead, she carried the dog out to the kitchen. Genevieve considered it her right to be carried everywhere. Everyone in the family obliged her.

Toni's mother was peering into the oven. "Looks good, if I do say so myself," she murmured.

Toni set the dog on the floor. Genevieve looked mildly offended, but she went over to her blanket and plopped down.

"Mom," Toni said, "this is more complicated than you think. The way I understand it, Hollan is pretty upset about Kyle leaving the partnership. According to Jackie, he's even talking about postponing the wedding. For Jackie's sake, we should encourage Kyle to go *back* to the partnership—not design me a house, of all things."

Marianne rummaged around in the refrigerator, but she seemed to be giving the subject a lot of thought. At last she emerged with some mustard greens and endive. "Toni, you know I love your sister, but maybe Jackie will have to take care of herself on this one. A very attractive, very interesting man has appeared in your life. Not to mention that he has initiative. If he wants to design a house for you...I'd go with it. For goodness' sake, if I were you, I wouldn't hang around with Dreary Dan when I could be discussing square footage and cathedral ceilings with the likes of Kyle Brennan.''

"So," Toni said, "that's why you're so gung ho about the house idea. You think it will make me fall into Kyle Brennan's arms. Sorry to disappoint you, but—''

"You'd think *someone* in this family would listen to me." Marianne plunked a jar of vinaigrette onto the counter with more force than necessary. Toni gave her mother a closer look.

"Mom, is everything all right?"

"Of course it is. Why wouldn't everything be all right?"

"Something seems to be bugging you," Toni said. "Is it work?"

"Work is fine."

Marianne was a high-school guidance counselor and had always professed to enjoy her job. Toni searched for other possibilities.

"It's not something with Dad, is it?"

"Your father is perfectly fine. He's planning our next trip, in fact. This time he wants to visit Nova Scotia.''

Toni's father had become something of a travel buff of late. A board member of the Heritage City Bank, he seemed to be casting about for diversion. He and Marianne had already spent an extended vacation in New Zealand.

Toni gave her mother another look. Marianne appeared as fit as ever. At fifty-two, her blond hair had scarcely faded; she wore it in a short bob that flattered her striking features. She jogged, played golf and had recently taken up weight training. Toni had always admired her mother's energy, but now a worrisome thought occurred.

"Mom, it's not something with your health, is it?"

"Will you stop? I've never felt better. There is nothing wrong, Toni." Marianne set the salad bowls out with a clatter. There was something wrong, Toni was sure of it.

"You'd better get it out," Toni said. "We're not leaving the kitchen till you do."

"Oh, for goodness' sake—" Marianne sighed. "Very well, then. I haven't told you this, honey, but they've offered your dad an early retirement, and he's going to take it. Then he wants us to travel full-time. The New Zealand trip was only a preview. Countless hours on planes and boats and trains…I don't think I can stand it!" Marianne looked frazzled just talking about it.

"Mom, maybe you should tell Dad how you're feeling."

"Don't you think I've tried? He simply won't listen. He sees us as world explorers. Toni, I'm all for new sights...but sometimes I'd just like to stay home with the dog."

Toni wished she had some advice to offer her mother. Apparently, Dad had latched on to too much of a good thing—that could definitely be a problem.

When they all sat down to dinner a short time later, it did seem that Dad expounded more than necessary on the New Zealand trip. Kyle, however, didn't appear to mind. He continued getting along just fine with both her parents.

Toni could only feel grateful when the meal was finished, and she finally had a private moment with Kyle. Her father began helping her mother to clear the dishes, and Toni escorted Kyle out to the back patio. The shadows of evening enveloped them, but the blooms lingering in the autumn garden were just visible: the delicate red and white of dianthus, the glossy pink of begonias, the bright yellow and orange of marigolds. Toni sat down in a wicker lawn chair, while Kyle leaned against one of the awning rails.

"I wonder if you have any more surprises," Toni remarked.

"I think we have them all covered. I quit my job,

I sign on to design your house, I have dinner with your parents...yep, that's about it.''

"You haven't signed on yet," Toni muttered. "Kyle—what *is* all this about you leaving the partnership? How could you do it so suddenly?"

"It's not sudden, Toni." All humor had vanished from Kyle's tone. "It's been coming on for a long time. I knew I needed something different in my life. I just wasn't sure what."

Toni shook her head. "And then yesterday, according to Jackie, you saw the light—"

"I saw a house, Toni. Your house...right up there on the bluff where we had the picnic. That's the place for it. Do you know how long it's been since I felt like this? Inspired, if that's what you want to call it.''

Toni sensed the excitement in Kyle—the enthusiasm. She heard it in his voice, saw it in the way he couldn't seem to stand still. He walked across the patio, then back again.

"Inspired," he repeated. "Maybe that's the only word for it. I haven't felt like this since Hollan and I started out. There's something about your land up there, Toni, something that demands just the right house...hell, I stayed up half the night, working on sketches. Nothing ready to show yet, but I'll get there..."

Toni felt as if Kyle had jumped aboard a roller-coaster ride, and pulled her along with him.

"Kyle, I appreciate the fact that you're...enthused. But you *are* moving too damn fast. I keep telling you I don't want you in my life, and you keep showing up anyway! And every time you get in deeper. I just don't—I don't want it, that's all." She stood restlessly. "I'm ticked at you, too," she added. "You didn't come talk to *me* about a blasted house. Instead you showed up here. You knew I wouldn't be amenable, so you figured pitch the idea to my parents. Very clever. And very high-handed—"

"You're a lawyer, Toni," he said imperturbably. "You've probably been high-handed on occasion."

"Assertive, maybe. Even aggressive. But not over-bearing. *Not* domineering and just plain arrogant—"

"Guilty as charged," said Kyle. "If building a dream house for you is arrogant, that's me."

"Dream house," Toni echoed. "Don't be ridiculous."

"Can't you see it, too?" he murmured. "Can't you imagine it? Up there on the ridge...the house you've always secretly wanted."

His voice was impossibly seductive. Toni tried not to be influenced, but somehow she did see it. A home all her own, up there at her special "lookout" place. She'd have a perfect view of her own wildflower meadow, and beyond, the vineyards and orchards of the valley...

"Nonsense," she said. "I've already told you, my life is here in Heritage."

"Up north...that's your real heritage."

She didn't want to listen. "If you want to design houses—fine, Kyle. Just go design someone else's."

"Inspiration's one of those things. When you haven't had it in a long while, and you finally feel it— you don't treat it cavalierly. You give it a little respect, and that means following where it leads you."

There it was again—the intensity in his voice, the conviction. She recognized the type of excitement she hadn't felt for her own work in quite some time. Toni almost started to envy him, until she remembered that Kyle Brennan was interfering in her life, big time.

"What about Hollan?" she demanded. "Doesn't it bother you at all that you've walked out on your own partner?"

"Hollan's an adult. He can take care of himself. And he knows that I haven't been happy. He knows some type of change has been coming."

"But don't you see?" Toni protested. "He really *is* disturbed about it. Jackie says he even wants to postpone the wedding, that's how bad it is—"

"Toni," Kyle said quietly. "Has it occurred to you that maybe Hollan is using this as an excuse?"

Toni stared at him in the light spilling from the house. "Are you saying Hollan doesn't want to marry my sister?"

"I'm saying he loves her, but maybe the thought of marriage scares the hell out of him. Any delay might be welcome right now."

"Poor Jackie," Toni said. "I've never seen her like this about a guy."

Kyle came to stand in front of her, and took her hand. His touch sent a quiver of warmth through her.

"Toni, this isn't about Jackie, or Hollan. It's about you and me. Why are you so afraid to let me in your life?"

She gazed into his eyes. They seemed a deeper brown than ever, full of mysteries she could not know. She tried to slip her hand away, but Kyle wouldn't let her go. He drew her closer to him. And then, without another word, he bent his head and kissed her.

## CHAPTER SIX

THE GIRL SEEMED very, very young to Toni—young and fragile, despite her stony expression. Sarah Martin's light brown hair was pulled back in a ponytail. She wore no makeup, no jewelry, no feminine trifle of any kind. Such were the results of being confined to jail, perhaps, but Toni had the feeling that Sarah's lack of adornment was more than temporary. Her plainness seemed deliberate. Sarah Martin had just turned eighteen, and she was accused of killing her own child.

Toni sat down across from Sarah in the interview room of the county jail. This place, too, was stripped of any adornment, as if to imply that only the basics would be dealt with here. Innocence or guilt. Hope or despair.

Toni placed a file on the table and opened it. She'd already studied the contents, but she went over the details one more time. Then she glanced at Sarah.

"I want to hear your version," she said.

The girl's expression did not change. "It tells you everything right there, doesn't it?" Her voice was as stony as her face.

"Not everything," Toni said. "It tells me what the police and the paramedics found when they came to your house. But it doesn't really tell me what happened before."

Sarah didn't answer. She turned away from Toni. She had a delicate profile; no severity in manner or tone could change that. Reports were that Sarah Martin had not cried at all in the two days since her child's death. She hadn't wept for her little boy, and she hadn't spoken about him.

"Sarah," Toni said, "I'm going to be your lawyer. You need to tell me exactly what happened Monday night."

"I didn't ask for a lawyer."

"I'm with the public defender's office," Toni said. "I've been assigned to your case."

Sarah gave her a disinterested look. "Assigned...you don't want to be here, do you? And I don't want you."

Admittedly, Toni hadn't been thrilled about this case. A child only a year and a half old, who had died from injuries associated with a severe shaking. A young mother accused of inflicting this abuse, and then very calmly calling the police to say her little boy was dead. No, Toni hadn't been too sympathetic about her newest client when she'd read the file.

Now, however, she was sitting across from Sarah Martin. The girl's stoic behavior got to her. If nothing else, Toni wanted to see some emotion—any emotion. Grief, anger…anything.

"Sarah, tell me what happened on Monday," she said again. "Start at the beginning."

"Please go away." Sarah spoke these words in a monotone.

"Your parents are very worried about you."

No response, not even a flicker. Toni read the file again. Sarah Martin lived at home with her mother and stepfather. At the time of the child's death, both had been absent from the house. Only Sarah had been there, Sarah and her little boy.

"I can't help you unless you tell me what happened Monday night," Toni said. "Sarah…what about your baby's father?"

"His name is Richard Johnston." Sarah spoke almost automatically. "He left town a long time ago. He doesn't want anything to do with me. He's gone." She stood and moved toward the door as if seeking escape. It was locked, of course. Right now Sarah Martin wasn't going anywhere.

"Sarah—" Toni tried again.

The girl lowered her head. But then, after a moment, she raised it again. She stared right at Toni. "He's gone," she said in that wooden voice. "He's gone, and nothing else matters. Don't you see? If he's gone…I don't care what happens to me."

SKETCHBOOK TUCKED under his arm, Kyle knocked on the door of Toni's apartment. He didn't have any illusions—he knew she wouldn't be happy to see him. But he'd had to come here this evening anyway. He hadn't been able to stop himself. He'd already stayed away a week, and he figured that was long enough.

He knocked again. The door swung open, and Toni gazed out at him with the skeptical expression she seemed to reserve just for him.

"Kyle…you're not here for a repeat performance, are you?"

He knew she was talking about that kiss last week at her parents' house. He hadn't planned on that kiss. The moment had seemed right, that was all… Toni had seemed right. Now his gaze traveled over her. She was wearing jeans. The soft denim conformed itself to her curves in all the right places. And her T-shirt…that was nice, too.

"Kyle, it shouldn't have happened."

"Yeah, I seem to remember you saying that right afterward."

Toni had a determined look. "I don't want it to happen again."

"If I promise not to kiss you," he said, "will you let me in?"

She ignored the question. Instead, she frowned at his sketchbook. "What's that?"

"I have a few ideas ready to show you. Very preliminary, but I wanted you to see them."

"Kyle, you have to give it up. I didn't agree to let you design a house for me."

"You didn't say yes. But you didn't say no, either."

She shook her head. "Kyle...I can't really discuss it with you right now. Dan's coming by to pick me up in an hour, and I have a ton of things to do before then."

The disappointment Kyle felt took him off guard. "Damn, I forgot. Wednesdays and Saturdays, right?"

Toni gave him a sour glance. "Yes, Wednesdays and Saturdays. So you can see that I'm a little busy."

He considered his options. Giving in to Dan Greene didn't seem to be one of them. "I did drive all the way down here," he said. "Five minutes, Toni. Give me that much."

He could see her wavering. She was probably thinking about booting him back to San Francisco, but at last she gave a shrug.

"Oh, what the hell," she said, opening the door wider. "Five minutes."

He stepped inside her living room. Despite the small space, he was greeted by the sense of spaciousness he remembered. Toni had a way with decorating—shame to waste it on an apartment.

"I'll look at your ideas," she said, "but that's it.

I'm not promising anything.'' She sat down on her antique sofa, gazing at him expectantly.

He couldn't explain it, but suddenly he felt as nervous as he had years ago when he'd landed his first internship with an architectural firm. He'd wanted to make a good impression—more than that, he'd wanted to bowl the firm over with his ideas. He'd succeeded then, but he suspected Toni Shaw wouldn't be so easily won.

He sat beside her, opened the sketchbook and handed it to her. She studied the first page, then the second...then the third. And he studied Toni. He could tell she was making an effort to remain impartial. But then he saw it, just the barest hint of a smile. It happened while she was examining the last sketch he'd made: a rounded wall made entirely of glass, intended to look out over the valley. The smile remained, and he knew he'd gotten to her.

"At first I was thinking one story," he said. "But it has to be two. Next page—that's the staircase I have in mind. It has to draw your attention, but not be too dramatic. Nothing worse than an overly dramatic staircase..."

It seemed he'd spoken too soon. Toni snapped the sketchbook shut and returned it to him.

"Kyle, I've already figured out that you're a very talented architect. Office buildings, houses—whatever you do, I'm sure it'll work out great. But as for me, I'm just not in the market.''

He'd seen that hint of a smile. Maybe he hadn't won her over yet...but he hadn't lost yet, either.

''Are my five minutes up?'' he asked.

''Yes, but you can stay another five,'' she said grouchily. ''One cup of coffee, and that's it. You're out of here.''

''Fair enough.''

She went to the kitchen, and he followed her. The cabinets were painted white, with glass doors and old-fashioned porcelain knobs. The stove and refrigerator were old-fashioned, too—white and chrome, the kind that cost a fortune just so you could look as if you'd inherited your grandmother's appliances. Toni had clearly indulged.

''You do the cabinets yourself?'' he asked.

''I made a deal with my landlord. He tore out the old cabinets, I put in the new ones. Seemed like a fair trade.''

''Not really. When you put money into something you don't own, you're just pouring it down the drain. You bought the appliances, too, didn't you?''

''I can take those with me...that is, if I ever decide to move. And I don't see that happening anytime soon,'' she added pointedly. ''I like this place.'' She put the kettle on to boil. ''You'll have to settle for instant,'' she said. ''We don't have time for brewed.''

He grinned. "We don't?"

"No, Kyle...we don't." She stood at the counter and folded her arms.

He tried to think of a way to prolong his five minutes. "How's work?" he asked.

"The usual. Except...I got a new case today."

He settled down on a stool across the counter. "Tell me about it."

"It's sad. An eighteen-year-old girl accused of killing her own baby."

"Did she do it?" Kyle asked.

"Good question. Everyone thinks she did. She seems so hard, Kyle. She says her boyfriend left her, and who knows...maybe that sent her into a rage. Maybe she took it out on that poor little boy of hers..." Toni's voice trailed off, and she appeared deep in thought. Kyle liked watching her think. Her face was more expressive than she probably liked; he saw puzzlement and concern and a few other emotions he couldn't define so well. Then he just relaxed and enjoyed the way she looked. The dark gold hair tumbling around her face, the fact that her eyes seemed more blue than green just now... Toni Shaw was a whole lot more beautiful than she realized.

"Damn," she muttered now under her breath. "This girl, Sarah, she won't cooperate with me one bit. She says she doesn't care what happens to her. Maybe she really is hard...but you know what she reminds me of, Kyle? She reminds me of a pond that's been frozen over all winter. Ice on top, thick ice, and everyone's forgotten what's underneath.'' The kettle whistled, and Toni reached over to turn off the stove. "She said something I'm still trying to figure out. She said, 'he's gone, and nothing else matters.' But here's the question. Was she talking about her boyfriend, or her son? It's been bothering me."

Toni lapsed into silence again as she brought out mugs, cream, sugar and the instant coffee. Kyle liked watching her move. He found that he liked a lot of things about Toni Shaw. She perched on a stool beside him, and they drank their coffee in what seemed a companionable silence. Or maybe it was just that Toni had chosen to forget his presence. She remained deep in thought, and he suspected she was still mulling over her case. That was fine with him. He wanted to go on sitting here with her, stretching out his five minutes.

Toni wasn't going to let him get away with it, though. Suddenly she set her mug down and glanced at her watch.

"I really do have to get ready," she told him.

Regretfully he set down his own mug and stood. "I'm going to leave those sketches with you. Just have another look at them."

"Kyle, I'm not going to take you on as my own personal architect. I don't know how to make that any clearer."

"Okay, I hear you. But I'd like your opinion on the sketches, so I'm going to leave them anyway."

She didn't say no. He took that as a promising sign. They'd reached the front door, and Kyle debated how to say good-night to her. Shaking hands seemed a little too formal. He allowed his gaze to travel over her once more, lingering on her mouth.

"Kyle," she said, a warning note in her voice.

He took a step nearer. She held her ground. He took another step. She stared at him defiantly. He lowered his head, almost brushed his lips against hers...

She slipped away from him. "Dammit," she said, her voice unsteady, "you promised."

"Did I?" he murmured. He saw how a flush had risen in her cheeks. It made her look even prettier than before.

She put more distance between them. "I can't do this, Kyle. I just can't."

The regret stirred in him again. "Does this guy matter so much to you?"

"Dan is...a very dependable person—"

"I'm not talking about Dan. I'm talking about the other guy. Greg, you said his name was. Are you still in love with him, Toni?"

She drew in her breath. "No!"

She'd spoken too quickly, too defensively. "I'm no expert," Kyle said, "but you still seem to have some feelings for him."

"No, I don't." Her voice had gone tight. "You can't let someone hurt you like that, and then turn around and forgive."

"So," Kyle said. "He asked you to forgive him."

She swiveled away as if to hide her expression. "He asked. I said no. End of story."

She went briskly to the sofa and picked up his sketchbook. "Please take this," she said. "I don't think it's such a good idea for you to leave it here. I'm sorry, Kyle."

"You're firing me?" he asked, keeping his tone light.

"I never hired you in the first place." In order to hand him the sketchbook, she had to walk over to him again. He gazed at her.

"I see it in your eyes," he murmured. "That expression...the sad one."

"I'm not sad. I'm perfectly happy."

"Not from where I stand." He stepped toward her. She stared at him as defiantly as ever, but she didn't move away. He took her in his arms, and he kissed her.

At first it was not a successful endeavor. The sketchbook was angled awkwardly between them. And Toni had stiffened, as if determined to resist him. He considered giving up the effort. But then, with a sigh of relinquishment, Toni leaned against him. The sketchbook was getting crushed. He didn't mind. He just wanted to go on holding Toni in his arms, tasting the sweetness of her. She ran her hands up over his shoulders, molded herself closer to him. That felt good. Everything about her felt good...

A loud knock came at the front door. Toni sprang away from Kyle, the sketchbook falling to the floor.

"Oh, Lord," she whispered. "What am I doing? That's Dan." She glanced at her watch. "Except that Dan's never this early." The pretty flush had stolen over her cheeks again.

"I wouldn't mind meeting your Dan Greene," Kyle said.

"He's not *my* Dan Greene—" She gave him a beleaguered look just as the knock sounded again, more demanding this time. Muttering something under her breath, Toni went to the door, unlocked it and swung it open.

Jackie practically came flying into the apartment.

"Toni, I'm so glad you're here! I have something terribly important to tell you—" She saw Kyle. "Oh. It's you." She examined him disdainfully. "I don't suppose it matters if *you're* here. You'll know soon enough, I'm sure."

"Jackie, what is it?" Toni asked. "You seem agitated."

Jackie strode to the center of the room, then faced both Kyle and Toni.

"I have wonderful news," she announced. "I'm pregnant. I'm going to have Hollan's baby!"

And, with that, Jackie Shaw burst into tears.

THERE'D BEEN A TIME when construction sites had fascinated Kyle. All the noise and action—drills thrumming, cranes looming, girders clanging. Today, however, he felt no excitement.

"You called me out here for an emergency," Kyle told Hollan. "Where's the damn emergency?"

Hollan's face took on an offended look underneath the hard hat. "Man, you said you wouldn't leave me in the lurch. You said you'd follow through on all ongoing projects—"

"I said it, I meant it. But where's the damn emergency?" Kyle repeated. He had to raise his voice to be heard over the usual commotion. They were walking along the eastern perimeter of the site. The complex was going up in a town not all that far from Heritage City. Too bad how Kyle's thoughts kept turning toward Heritage these days.

"Max wanted to go over the specs with us," Hollan said.

"Max never wants to go over the specs. He handles everything just fine without us." They'd worked with Max Grainger's construction crew plenty of times before. "What's this really about, Hollan? Except why am I even asking…it's Jackie, right? She's driving you crazy."

They'd reached a spot where they could almost hear themselves talk. Hollan took off his hard hat and wiped the sweat from his forehead.

"You don't understand. Listen, man. She's pregnant!"

"So I hear," Kyle said.

"Wait a minute. When did you hear?"

"Last night," Kyle said. "Jackie showed up at her sister's place and made the big announcement. I was going to call to congratulate you, but then I got your message about the emergency."

"It *is* an emergency. What the hell am I going to do? Kids…babies." Hollan sounded as if he was talking about aliens.

"Maybe what you should do is convince your fiancée you really want the baby. She was pretty upset last night. She says your initial reaction was less than enthusiastic."

"She told you that?"

"In so many words. I had to leave before I got the full story." In reality, the two Shaw sisters had unceremoniously requested his departure. Jackie had made clear that, as Hollan's friend, he was considered the enemy. Toni had simply made clear that his time had expired.

"Jackie doesn't have anything to worry about,"

Hollan said lugubriously. "I already let her know I'm going to do the honorable thing. I'll go ahead with the wedding."

"I'm sure your enthusiasm overwhelmed her." Kyle sat down on a pile of bricks and took off his own hard hat.

Hollan sat down, too, hunching forward as he propped his elbows on his knees. "She just dropped this on me, you know? Out of the blue."

"Yeah, well, you had a little something to do with it."

"I thought we were being careful," Hollan muttered. "She told me she was taking care of it, anyway."

Kyle decided he was hearing more than he wanted to know. "These things happen," he said.

"What if she did it on purpose? You know, so she could snare me..."

Hollan obviously wasn't thinking too logically right now. Maybe it was the shock.

"Hollan, figure it out. You asked *her* to marry *you*. Little over two months ago. If I remember, you had to do some convincing before she said yes. You didn't get cold feet until afterward."

"Right, right," Hollan said distractedly. "Okay, so it was an accident. My whole life has to change because of an accident?"

Kyle had been friends with Hollan for a long time. But today his friend was getting on his nerves.

"You told me Jackie was the best you could ever have. Okay, so marriage is a little daunting. Parenthood…daunting, too. But if you love her, why not jump in and go for it? The two of you'll swim together."

He should have used a different image, because now Hollan got a nostalgic look. "Swimming…that was a pretty good time, wasn't it? Both you and me on the team…both of us free. Remember those girls in Newport Beach…"

Kyle didn't particularly care to remember his college years. If he'd been a little wild back then, he'd gotten it out of his system.

"Hollan, just tell Jackie you love her. Tell her you want to have a family with her."

"Sure, I'll do the honorable thing," Hollan said dourly. "I'll marry her."

His friend obviously hadn't got the point. Kyle stood and walked ahead. Hollan caught up to him.

"Okay," Hollan said. "You've had a week to think it over. You don't have to leave the partnership."

"Yes, I do," Kyle said. "It's time for both of us to move on."

"Hell, I lose my best buddy and find out I'm going to be a father, all practically the same week—"

"We're still friends, Hollan."

"Yeah, well, don't get mushy," Hollan said in his best sarcastic mode. "You know what I mean—things aren't going to be the same."

"They can't be. They have to change. People get married, have kids—that type of thing."

"You talk," said Hollan. "But I don't see you getting married. I don't see you having kids."

No argument there. Kyle wasn't exactly moving ahead in the family department. As far as careers went...he'd chucked the partnership, only to find out his services as home designer were not yet in demand. Too bad he had only one house in mind right now. Toni's house.

"So what's with the sister?" Hollan asked.

"Nothing," Kyle said.

"Nothing? You said you were at her place last night."

"Not by invitation."

"Bummer," Hollan said after a moment.

Kyle knew there were plenty of reasons why he shouldn't even be thinking about Toni Shaw. For starters, his career was up in the air. Sure, Toni was the one client he wanted right now, but they told you never to get involved with your clients.

There was another reason. No matter what Toni said, she still had feelings for some guy named Greg. She still had unfinished business.

It was a bummer, all right.

# CHAPTER SEVEN

TONI WROTE a few words on the chalkboard that hung in her office. Then she stood back and took a look. The name SARAH MARTIN stood out in bold block letters across the top. Underneath she'd jotted another name, in smaller letters: Jeremy Edward Martin. An imposing name for a year-and-a-half-old boy. A little boy who had died.

In a different color of chalk, Toni had scribbled the rest of it. Time of death—location of body—Sarah's phone call to the police—potential whereabouts of baby's father. It was all very stark, very grim.

"Hello, Toni."

Kyle's voice...

She swiveled and there he was, standing in the doorway of her office. Almost a week had gone by since he'd come to her apartment. Why was it that every time she saw the man, she felt as if she had to catch her breath?

She made a great effort to frown at him. "Kyle, you know what my next question is going to be."

He gave her that smile of his, the one that made her

feel as if she wanted to kick off her shoes and curl up in his arms. "Right," he said. "What am I doing here."

"Okay," she said. "So what are you doing here?"

"It's almost lunchtime. And I owe you lunch."

"Kyle, you don't owe me anything—"

"Yes, I do," he said. "After the way I've disrupted your life lately—you know, trying to design you a house, and all—I figured I should make it up to you."

She stared at him in exasperation. "Let me get this straight. Your idea of making up for disruption…is to come down here and disrupt my life all over again—"

"Yes, that's the idea."

She saw the humor in his eyes. "Kyle…"

"I really would like to talk to you, Toni. I have some things to say I think you ought to hear. Why not do it over lunch?"

She wished she had a good answer to that. She glanced at her chalkboard. Kyle gave it a perusal, too, and somehow she felt as if she had to explain.

"I've been using chalkboards ever since law school," she said. "They help me to think. There's something about big letters on the wall—helps put things in perspective, I guess."

Kyle nodded. "The creative process."

"Some people don't think lawyers are very creative people."

"Solving a case—pretty creative, if you ask me,"

he said. "That's what you're trying to do, isn't it, solve this case of yours? The girl accused of killing her child…"

Toni rubbed the chalk dust from her fingers. "My boss says there's nothing to solve. He says all the evidence points to Sarah Martin, and we should just try to get the best deal for her we can—then on to the next customer."

"You think different."

She shook her head. "I don't know what to think right now. I'm doing everything I can to locate the baby's father. I have a name, and not much else to go on. But something tells me to keep at it."

She glanced at Kyle, and saw that he seemed to be listening to her with genuine interest. She wished she could say the same thing for her boss—*he* didn't even want to hear about her doubts.

"I should know better," she said, "but I'm going to take you up on your invitation. Except for one thing. I pick the venue."

"Fair enough," he said.

She grabbed her briefcase and they went out to the parking lot. Toni saw Kyle's convertible parked in one of the spaces.

"We'll take my car," she said.

"Fair enough."

She gave him a sharp glance, then led the way to her hatchback—another survivor of her law-school days. She got in the driver's seat, Kyle took the passenger side. Toni had the feeling he wasn't really the passenger type. No doubt he was happier being the take-charge type, the one behind the wheel. But they were on her turf now, and she meant to keep the advantage.

She drove out of the lot and down Main Street. Heritage City was in the throes of its latest renovation project. The turn-of-the-century bank on the corner of Main and Sixth was being refaced, and new street lamps were being put in all the way down to Copper.

"This town's a little fickle—constantly trying to hold on to the past while chasing after the future," Toni said. "I don't think it knows where it wants to be."

"I like the place," Kyle said.

"We're not much compared to San Francisco," she told him.

She could feel his gaze on her, lingering, and she found it difficult to concentrate on driving.

What she really had to do was find a restaurant. She wanted an ordinary atmosphere, something down-to-earth and prosaic. She slowed as they approached Jay's Grill. That was where she went every Saturday night with Dan...

She braked, but then changed her mind.

"What's the matter?" Kyle asked.

"Nothing." Nothing except that five minutes later

they ended up at a small, intimate Italian restaurant in what Heritage liked to think of as its chic district. Crisp white tablecloths, watercolors of Rome and Venice and Palermo on the walls, opera music playing ever so softly in the background—Toni could simply not have chosen a more romantic atmosphere if she'd tried. So why on earth had she brought Kyle here?

"I haven't been here in a long time," she said, as if that would somehow excuse her lack of judgment.

"I like it," Kyle said.

"You can't like everything about Heritage City."

"Why not?" he asked, smiling at her again. It seemed they were sitting far too close together. Of course, the table wasn't very big, so they *had* to sit close together...

Toni opened her menu and tried to focus on the food. "You said you had something to talk to me about," she reminded him.

"Not on an empty stomach," he cautioned. "Antonia, never have a serious discussion when you're hungry."

"So it's serious, is it?"

"Very serious." The humor glimmered in his eyes.

"I'm starting to suspect you don't have a thing to talk to me about."

"All in due time, Antonia. First we try the *pomodori* and the *anelletti*..."

Good heavens, did the man speak Italian, too? The

way those words came off his tongue, sounding so rich and sensuous, Toni had to retreat behind her menu and tell herself to get control.

But she couldn't help herself. She did end up or-dering the *pomodori* and the *anelletti*, right along with him: tomatoes in caper sauce, and pasta with eggplant. Not to mention the mussels with lemon, the mince croquettes and the chocolate pear cake.

"You can't accuse us of being hungry anymore," Toni said at last. "So if you really *do* have something to talk to me about...now's the time."

"I suppose you're right. Now's the time. Toni, I've finished the design for your house." He held up his hand as if to stave off her automatic protest. "Hear me out first," he said. "I'm not asking you to look at the design. I'm finished with it, and I'm going to put it away. I'm not going to try selling you on the idea anymore."

Toni studied Kyle. She could tell he was serious, and she struggled with the odd sense of letdown she was feeling. She waited for him to continue.

"Toni, these last few weeks it's been great to feel inspired. Creating something that I had to get down on paper right away, waking up in the middle of the night with a new idea...yeah, it's been great. It's made me remember that I felt the same way when I started out with Hollan. Excited, new ideas always coming to mind. We both felt that way, I think. But then the worst thing possible happened to us."

He paused, and she found herself leaning toward him a bit. "What happened, Kyle?"

He grimaced. "We got successful, that's what happened. More demand for our work than we could handle. We threw ourselves into it, worked the long hours day after day. That made us even more successful. Of course, somewhere along the way we lost the excitement. Sure, maybe the inspiration was still there—you have to have it, in our business—but it got buried beneath all that production."

"Well, now you've unburied it, haven't you? You've regained your inspiration."

"I wish it was that easy," he said. "I indulged myself on that design for you. I made it completely my own vision. Best time I ever had. But I'm smart enough to realize it's not the kind of thing I can replicate very often."

"You can design houses for other clients," she said. "Lots of other clients, I'd bet, given your reputation and your talent. You'd be very successful—"

He gave her a wry look. "And I'd be churning out houses the way I used to churn out office buildings. I can't go that route again, Toni. I have to find a better solution. Until I do, I'm glad I had the chance to design a house that fulfilled my own vision, no one else's. And the fact that it led nowhere—it will never get built—perhaps that's the best part of all. I did it just for the inspiration. Maybe I'll frame a picture of it and hang it up on the wall—just to remind me what creating really feels like.''

"But, Kyle, don't you want to see the house become a reality? Don't you want to see it up there on my land?''

"At first I did. But now I realize you need your own vision—not mine. If you ever do decide to put a house on that land...tell the architect what *you* want, Toni.''

She was battling a letdown, all right. "At least you could let me see the design,'' she said. "All you showed me last week were a few sketches. I'd be interested in seeing the finished idea.''

"No,'' Kyle said. "I'm letting you off the hook. I shouldn't have put pressure on you. Like I said, Toni, that design isn't going to solve my career problems. I was wrong to make you think it would.''

"So,'' she said, trying for a light tone. "You're firing *me* now.'' She was experiencing the most alarming curiosity. What did his final design look like? The sketches she'd seen had enticed her, but they'd only been bits and pieces. A wall of glass...an intriguing alcove...a hint of a sunroom...

Out loud she said, "It's for the best. A house on Grandpa's land wouldn't solve anybody's problems.''

"Definitely not,'' he agreed.

"Well...I suppose it's time to get going," she said.

Kyle summoned the waiter, paid the bill and then escorted Toni outside. They got into the hatchback and drove back to her office. Afterward, she walked with Kyle to his car.

"Thanks for lunch," she said awkwardly. "It was...nice of you."

"Hey, my pleasure."

"I suppose you're headed back to San Francisco," she said.

He nodded. "I still have to check into the office now and then. Dissolving a partnership isn't something you can do overnight."

"Sounds like you're busy, then."

"I'm keeping myself occupied," he said. "A career crisis has its own agenda."

Why couldn't she just let him go? Why was she trying to delay?

"Oh, look," she finally blurted. "I'm taking some time off work this afternoon. I promised Mom I'd show up for career day at her high school. She's a guidance counselor, and...it's career day, that's all. I'm wondering—do you want to come with me, Kyle?"

"Career day," he repeated solemnly. "You're thinking maybe I'll get some pointers for my crisis?"

"On second thought, forget it. I know it's ridiculous—"

"Not so fast," he said. "Let's examine this. Maybe you were asking me on a date just now, and I didn't recognize it."

"No, I was not asking you on a date. It's career day, for crying out loud—"

He grinned. "Sure, I'll come, even if it's not a date."

But that only left Toni with more questions. Why was she so glad he'd said yes? Why was she so glad she didn't have to say goodbye to him—not just yet?

TWO HOURS LATER, Toni stood in the gymnasium of Heritage High, arranging cookies on paper plates. Kyle was beside her, pouring punch into paper cups.

"Back on the food line," he said with good-natured cynicism. "I never figured this career-day thing would take me back to the first career I ever had—working the food lines at my junior-high cafeteria. It was a penance I served for skipping English class three days in a row. I got to spend my lunch hour in an apron and a chef's cap, spooning out the hash."

Toni attached herself to Kyle's arm. "I'll bet you were cute in your little hat. Maybe you should have been the one to give a talk for career day."

"No thanks. I've never been one for the spotlight. Your sister, however, seems to thrive on it."

Toni came to Jackie's defense—something of a habit, where her sister was concerned. "I think Jackie did a very good job today. I've never seen so many interested teenagers. Broadcast journalism seems to be a very popular career.''

"Okay, so the kids liked her," he conceded. "But I thought maybe you were going to get up there, too, and give your spiel."

Toni shook her head. "What, the thrills of lawyering? If you want to know the truth, Mom asked me to do it. She thought it would be dandy to have her two daughters speak together. But I just couldn't bring myself to give in. You might recall I've been having my own career crisis. I couldn't make myself tell those kids that law school is the be-all, end-all. So instead I volunteered to head the refreshment table."

Kyle helped himself to one of the punches he'd poured. "Maybe there's something else going on," he said. "Maybe you're too used to giving your sister the limelight—and she's too used to taking it."

Toni stopped right in the middle of alternating peanut-butter cookies with raisin-oatmeal. She stared at Kyle. "That's absurd. I'm not interested in the limelight. And if that's Jackie's calling...well, that's just Jackie. Doesn't have anything to do with me."

Kyle helped himself to one of the oatmeal cookies and looked philosophical. "I get it," he said. "Lawyering is supposed to be your chance to make a mark. Something different than your sister chose, so she won't feel too threatened—but meanwhile you get some limelight of your own."

Maybe it hadn't been such a good idea to invite Kyle along. His insights—if such they could be called—were profoundly irritating. But Toni didn't have the opportunity to argue. Teenagers began spilling into the gym from the assembly hall, many of them flocking in Jackie's wake. Toni studied her sister from across the room. Even though Jackie wasn't showing yet, it seemed that being pregnant suited her. She was lovelier than ever, her skin fresh, her long blond hair even more thick and shiny than before. Toni wondered uncomfortably if what Kyle said was true. Had she been drawn to law by more than interest, more than ideals? *Had* she seen it as a way, however subtle, to compete with Jackie?

But now Marianne Shaw appeared beside the refreshment table. "Mr. Brennan," she said, "how glad I am to see you. What a delightful surprise."

"It's Kyle—please."

"Very well then, Kyle. I'm so pleased Toni brought you." Marianne perused the two of them altogether too fondly, as if already hearing wedding bells.

"Mom, Kyle took me to lunch today, that's all, and—"

"Lunch. Isn't that nice."

"Exactly what Toni told me, Mrs. Shaw," Kyle said.

"Do call me Marianne. If we're going to be seeing this much of you, we can't be formal."

The situation was getting away from Toni. Then again, it had been getting away since the first minute she'd met Kyle Brennan.

"I wish I could stay and chat," Marianne said, "but I just saw a student I have to catch. I want her to enter a short-story contest, and the deadline's coming up." She waggled her fingers at Kyle and Toni, then hurried across the gym.

Toni watched her go. "Mom's really good at her job," she said. "She seems to love it, too."

"I like her," Kyle said. "Very pleasant lady, your mom. I think she and my mom would get along fine."

"Don't forget Aunt Eileen," Toni said just a bit caustically.

"Aunt Eileen, too."

She gazed at him suspiciously. "I could swear you're making that woman up. She just sounds so...so..."

"So Texan?" Kyle suggested gravely.

"Maybe that's it." She never quite knew when Kyle was being serious. He was the type of man who could keep you perpetually off balance, if you didn't watch out.

More distractions ensued, however. Hollan Nash the Third now appeared in the gym.

"I didn't know Hollan was going to be here," Kyle said.

"Neither did I."

Jackie seemed to be making an effort to ignore Hollan. She remained surrounded by admiring teenage boys, her back pointedly turned to her fiancé. Hollan stepped toward her. Even from this distance, Toni could swear she saw Jackie stiffen.

"Think they're going to blow?" Kyle asked.

"That's anybody's guess."

Hollan, however, already seemed to have given up. He came wandering over to Kyle and Toni.

"Hey, guys," he said apathetically. "I guess Jackie already told you."

"Told us—told us what?" Toni asked.

"The wedding's off again."

"Gee...I'm sorry," Toni said.

"What a surprise," Kyle said. "What is it this time?"

"The honcymoon," Hollan said darkly. "Can you believe it? We can't agree on the honeymoon. Where to go, what to do...can't agree on a damn thing."

Jackie extricated herself from the admiring teenage boys and came over to the refreshment table.

"Hello," she said frostily to Hollan.

"Hello."

"I don't see why you even bothered to come. You missed my speech."

"I tried to get here on time."

"Not hard enough, obviously." Jackie turned to Kyle and Toni. "I suppose he's told you. The wedding's off."

"Oh, hell, Jackie," Hollan said, sounding miserable. "Oh, hell, honey…"

She looked at him with tears shimmering in her eyes. "What are we going to do, Hollan?"

Hollan took Jackie into his arms, right there in the middle of the crowded gym. "I don't know," he said. "Let somebody else decide about the damn honeymoon. It's not worth us fighting all the time."

"Somebody else," Jackie murmured. "Somebody else decides…" She twisted around and gazed straight at Kyle and Toni. "What a wonderful idea!"

## CHAPTER EIGHT

RIDING A HORSE was a piece of cake.

Toni said as much to Kyle. "This is easy. If I'd known how easy, I would have taken up horseback riding a long time ago."

"You'll have one sore butt on the way back," he said.

Toni refused to have her illusions shattered. She was mounted on a very gentle mare named Lucinda. Except for a little jouncing around in the saddle, she was doing just fine.

She gazed ahead at Kyle. His mount was rather more rakish than hers—a bay gelding by the name of Buck. Kyle had picked him out personally. The animal seemed skittish, but Kyle kept him under control effortlessly. From here Toni had an unobstructed view of Kyle's backside in the saddle. He looked good on a horse. Very good...

"I can't believe we're doing this," she said. "Trying to find a honeymoon for my sister and your best friend. I mean, think about it. They actually want us to make the decision for them. Is that the craziest thing you ever heard?"

"Pretty crazy," he agreed.

"Explain again how they talked us into it," Toni said.

"I think it was the part where your sister started crying and said they'd never be able to get married unless we helped solve the honeymoon crisis, and if she didn't get married her baby would have a broken home before it was even born...I kind of lost track of the logic after that."

"I'll tell you what really got to me," Toni said. "It was when Jackie turned to me with that pitiful look and asked me to do it for the sake of the baby...my future niece or nephew... I tell you, I got tears in my own eyes. Except that logic *does* keep rearing its ugly little head. If two people can't even decide on their own honeymoon, how are they going to handle marriage and parenthood?"

"Got me there," Kyle said.

"So tell me again why we're doing this."

"Because," Kyle said, "you have a soft spot for your sister. And I...have a soft spot for you."

Toni flushed. "Don't start, Kyle."

"Seems we've already started," he said. "Maybe I'm just lookin' to move things along a little."

Toni wished he didn't sound so sexy when he got

that hint of Texas. "Kyle, you and I aren't going anywhere together," she said firmly.

He slowed until she caught up to him, and then the two horses clip-clopped side by side. "Antonia," he said, "maybe we're already somewhere. Look around. You...me...Honeymoon Ranch. What could be better?"

"What kind of place," muttered Toni, "has a name like Honeymoon Ranch?"

"A place," said Kyle, "where anything can happen."

She made the mistake of gazing into his eyes as they rode along, and her heartbeat did the predictable and accelerated. With an effort, she gazed forward again.

"I still can't believe we're doing this," she said. "Both Jackie and Hollan act as if once we find the perfect honeymoon for them, all their problems will be solved."

"Guess Hollan needs to latch on to something," Kyle said. "He loves your sister, but he's scared, too—scared of everything that's ahead."

"What about you?" Toni found herself asking. "If you were in the same position as Hollan...how would you feel?"

"If I found the right woman," he said, "I might be ready to take the plunge. Except I'd need to have my career in order first. No way would I take on a family without straightening that out.''

''How would you know she's the right woman?'' Toni asked.

''Good question. According to Hollan, I've never really fallen for anyone.''

''Never?''

''Never.''

''Maybe you're not missing anything,'' she said.

He slowed his horse to a halt, and Toni's mare stopped, too. He regarded her thoughtfully. ''So,'' he said, ''you're saying even if the right guy came along, you'd turn down marriage and kids.''

She twisted the reins in her fingers. ''The parenthood part, that I'd take. I know the parameters there. Basically, you love your kids with all your heart. If you do that, you can't go too terribly wrong. But the husband part...I'd pass on that. I don't have faith in that kind of love—the romantic kind. It doesn't last. You give so much...too much...and then it's gone...''

Kyle was still watching her, but Toni didn't want to discuss the topic anymore. She dug her heels into the mare's sides. ''C'mon, horse,'' she said. ''Hoof it.''

They followed the creek, while above them rose hills blanketed in chaparral. Butterflies floated lazily on the breeze and a bevy of quail made a bustling protest as the horses went by. Finally Kyle and Toni reached their destination, a log cabin tucked among pines and manzanita shrubs.

Kyle dismounted, then came to help Toni.

"I can do it myself," she said, only to find herself dangling awkwardly atop the horse. Kyle took hold of her and brought her safely to ground. He didn't let go, however, keeping his hands on her waist as he smiled at her.

"Kyle," she said suspiciously, "why did you *really* agree to this outing?"

"Because, Antonia, I like spending time with you."

She looked at him hard. "We are agreed this whole venture is strictly business."

"Honeymoon business," he said, bringing her just a little closer. She had to put her hands against his chest to steady herself.

"Darn it all, Kyle—"

"Business...but no funny business," he said with an air of disappointment. "I get it, Antonia." He released her. "Guess we'd better check out the digs."

They left the horses to graze on a grassy patch and went into the cabin. The manager of the place had provided them with a key so they could look around. The decor was pleasingly rustic: spindle chairs with rush seats, homespun curtains at the windows, an old-fashioned washstand complete with porcelain basin and pitcher. Toni sat down, taking a pencil and a few index cards from her shirt pocket.

"Okay," she said. "I thought we could use a point system for rating each honeymoon location. Up to twenty points for atmosphere, ten points for luxury— that type of thing. I have to admit, this place gets zero for luxury."

Kyle sat down on the plump bed dominating the center of the room. "I don't know…this mattress feels pretty luxurious. Want to come try it out?"

"No."

"An innocent request, Toni."

She ignored him and jotted some notes on one of her index cards. "As far as atmosphere, I'd give this place a rating of fifteen. It's very peaceful, and the scenery is beautiful, but I think it's a bit isolated for Jackie's taste. As for variety, I'd only give it a five. What does that leave? Some hiking trails, and some cabins seemingly in the middle of nowhere. Let's see…fifteen, five…that's twenty points."

"Gee, only twenty points," said Kyle. "Maybe we should consult Buck and Lucinda?"

"You can make fun of my system—or you can come up with one of your own."

Kyle stretched out on the bed. "I go more for the intuitive approach. How does a place feel to me? Can I relax? Do I feel like I can settle in for a while?"

Kyle looked as if he was settling into that mattress. "You're forgetting something," Toni said. "This isn't about how *you* feel. It's about how we think Jackie and Hollan will feel. So we have to come up with the most objective criteria possible.''

"Enter the point system.''

"Can you come up with something better?'' she asked.

He patted the mattress beside him. "Just try it out, Toni. This bed is damn comfortable—but don't take my word for it. How are you going to give it a point rating otherwise?''

The man was impossible. Toni set down her pencil and cards. She looked at Kyle. In his jeans and khaki shirt, he appeared completely at home. His scuffed cowboy boots dangled over the edge of the mattress, and the expression on his face was much too inviting.

"No way,'' said Toni.

Kyle didn't say anything at all. A few minutes later, Toni couldn't explain what possessed her. She went around to the other side of the bed and sat down gingerly on the mattress.

"I suppose it is comfortable,'' she said.

"You won't find out that way,'' he told her. "In my book, this is a ten-point mattress. Heck, make it fifteen.''

She gave up and against all her better judgment she stretched out on the mattress. She kept to the very edge, as far away as possible from Kyle.

"Okay, so it's comfortable,'' she said. "We add fifteen more points, and we're out of here.''

He turned his head to gaze at her. "Seems to me we haven't done the place full justice."

He rolled over on his side, propping his head in his hand. This brought him closer to her. However, she knew that if she scooted any farther away, she'd fall off the bed.

"Kyle..."

"I've come up with my own rating method," he said. "We pretend this is *our* honeymoon spot, and we try to figure out if we like it."

"Don't be ridiculous—"

"Use your imagination, Toni. Call it a little role-playing. Here's the scenario. We just got married. In fact, we eloped."

"No elopement," Toni said. "Weddings are important. The lace and the veil, the flower girls...the band playing sappy love songs at the reception." She listened to herself, amazed at what she was coming up with.

"I thought you didn't believe in weddings," Kyle said. "At least, you told me you didn't believe in husbands."

"I don't. But you said we were role-playing, and I'm...I'm just getting into the exercise. Besides, if you're reckless enough to get married in the first place, you might as well do it up with a bang."

"Okay, so I wanted to elope and you talked me out

of it. We did the church thing, with all the trimmings—''

"Back up a minute," Toni said. The bed really was
remarkably comfortable. "I want to know what kind
of engagement we had. Was it volatile or congenial?
Did you pamper or neglect? And how long did it last?
Three months—three years?"

"Nix on a long engagement," Kyle said. "We gave
it a couple of months, and then we tied the knot."

"I don't know," Toni said. "An engagement is a
time to get to know the other person. You don't want
to rush it. You have to figure out if you're truly com-
patible."

"Let me guess. The point system again. You chalk
up ten in my favor if I bring you flowers, minus five
if I forget to meet you for dinner—"

"Okay," Toni said. "Let's just say we had a whirl-
wind courtship and a traditional wedding. Now we've
shown up at the Honeymoon Ranch. And we're going
stir-crazy because there's nothing to do here."

"No…we don't need anything else to do. We have
plenty to occupy us." His gaze captured hers. The
laughter had vanished. Instead, all Toni saw was the
desire in his eyes…

"So much for role-playing," she said, moving away
from him so quickly that she almost *did* fall off the
bed. "I'm going to check out those hiking trails, just
for the sake of being thorough. You stay right

here…bye." She stood up, walked to the door and escaped outside. A clearly marked path led through the pines; Toni supposed that Honeymoon Ranch didn't want to lose any of its honeymooners in the wild.

She'd traveled for a few minutes at a good pace when Kyle caught up to her.

"You didn't have to come along," she said.

"Toni, why are you running from me?"

"I'm not running," she muttered. "I'm just making sure we give this locale a thorough investigation."

"I'm not the kind of person who would hurt you the way that other guy did. I wouldn't make promises, only to break them."

Toni stopped and turned to face him. "This isn't about Greg—"

"Yeah, I'd say it is. It's been about him all along. The guy betrayed you, broke your heart…and maybe, in spite of that, you're still in love with him."

Toni folded her arms against her body. She felt a surge of anger. "How could I possibly love a man who'd do *that* to me?"

"Logic has very little to do with love. The fact remains—you don't have closure on the guy."

Closure…she found the term maddening. "Like hell I didn't have closure! I threw him out the door, told him I never wanted to see him again. If *that's* not closure, I don't know what is—"

"Anybody who can still bring out this much emotion...definitely no closure."

"I wish," she said through clenched teeth, "you wouldn't keep using that word." She continued down the path. Kyle walked beside her. "You know something?" she said. "The only reason you like hanging around me is that your career is up in the air, and you don't have anything better to do. Right now you have too much time on your hands, Kyle, that's your problem. I seem to entertain you, and I suppose that keeps you from thinking about your real problems."

Apparently he didn't have any way to counter that. "I've always been a workaholic," he said. "And now, okay, I do have too much time on my hands."

"Exactly. So you're out looking for honeymoons with me, and flirting unforgivably, and—and generally driving me to distraction."

"At least I'm good for something," he said in a jocular tone. But she sensed the restlessness inside him, the discontent. Her anger drained away, leaving her with her own restlessness.

"Kyle, let's just...hike. They say exercise is good for helping people to work out their problems."

"Hasn't done me any good so far," he said. "I've been down to the gym, tried jogging, done laps at the pool. Still no answers."

"Who knows? Maybe Honeymoon Ranch is what you've been missing."

"I'm missing something," he said.

They hiked. They went up into the hills and down again. They went through pines and sycamores and some truly amazing redwoods. They kept moving for more than an hour before they turned back. And when they finally reached the cabin again, Kyle still looked restless, and Toni still felt as if she hadn't outwalked her troubles. Such as the way Kyle Brennan made her feel...

"It's hot," she said. "Let's cross this place off our list and get out of here."

"Try this," he said, gesturing toward the wash-stand. "If we want to say we gave the place a thorough investigation, we have to go all the way."

Toni leaned over the porcelain basin while Kyle poured water into her hands from the pitcher. She splashed her face. She had to admit there was something appealing about the old-fashioned method of doing things.

"You try it, too," she said. She poured from the pitcher for him. A few seconds later they both had cool, refreshing water dripping onto their shirts. Toni found a towel in the cabinet of the washstand and handed it to Kyle. He took it from her, but somehow ended up taking hold of her hand at the same time.

"Kyle, we really have to go."

"Not just yet, Toni." He gazed at her. She gazed back, even though every instinct warned her to turn away.

"It's not fair," she whispered.

"What's not fair?" He drew her closer.

"What you do to me…"

"What you do to me, Toni." He brought her into his arms and kissed her. She tasted the droplets of water on his lips. Cool drops of water…but inside her a warmth gathered, a heat she could not deny. With a sigh, a surrendering, she pressed herself closer to him. She wasn't thinking, wasn't listening to reason. She was just feeling, pouring herself into every sensation he aroused in her.

It was only a few short steps from the washstand to the bed. The towel dropped from Kyle's fingers as he sank onto the mattress with Toni. Her legs tangled with his, her arms reached up to bring him nearer again. He kissed her mouth, her throat.

"Lord," he said, his voice a husky murmur. "I've been wanting to do this since the first moment I saw you. The first moment you walked into that restaurant."

How could need flare so fiercely inside her? Only if it had been there all along, since the first moment too. He kissed her and caressed her until she had to whisper his name.

"Kyle…oh, Kyle…" It seemed all her better judgment had vanished, engulfed in the need. But then Kyle tugged her shirt impatiently from her jeans, moved his hand over her bare skin.

"No," she said, calling upon her last bit of common

sense. His hand stilled. "No," she repeated, more bleakly this time. And then, shirttails dangling, she scrambled off the bed and hurried out of the cabin.

KYLE PUNCHED the key that sent the file to the printer, then sat back, watching the pages roll out. After a moment, he glanced around his office. Correction: his former office. It was done in ultramodern—paintings on the walls that were so many slabs of pastel, a blocky glass desk he never felt comfortable about putting his feet on, an executive chair that looked as if it belonged on a spaceship. About a year ago, Hollan had been dating an interior decorator, and she'd taken over Nash and Brennan Architects for a time. Kyle and Hollan never had got the place back to normal.

Now Hollan appeared from his own office. "Didn't think I'd see you here today," he said.

"I told you I'd give you my update on the Plaza project."

"Yeah," Hollan said, "but I thought you'd be out looking for that...honeymoon." Hollan said the word as if it were a lethal weapon.

Kyle thought about the afternoon before last, when he and Toni had checked out the Honeymoon Ranch. They hadn't done too much honeymoon searching since then. The way Kyle saw it, they'd almost made love that afternoon. Toni, however, had "come to her senses," as she called it. He felt a stirring of regret.

Kyle regarded his friend. "How the heck did you

come up with an idea like that, anyway? Electing us as your own personal honeymoon committee.''

Hollan looked uncomfortable. ''I was just talking off the top of my head. I didn't know Jackie would take me up on it.''

''She took the idea and ran with it,'' Kyle grumbled. ''What kind of relationship do you and that girl have, anyway, that you can't decide on your own honeymoon?''

''I don't know what it is with her,'' Hollan said. ''Half the time I feel I can't live without her, and the other half...''

''Yeah, right, she drives you crazy,'' Kyle said.

''She says she wants the perfect honeymoon, but she won't take more than three days off for it. Three days, man. What good will that do us? But she's afraid if she's away from work any longer, they'll find somebody to replace her. How can she be so damn beautiful, and so damn insecure at the same time?'' Hollan asked. ''Women...''

''Don't blame the entire gender. You have plenty to do with this honeymoon nonsense. It's a damn fool idea,'' Kyle said, ''asking somebody else to find your honeymoon.''

''Don't I know it,'' Hollan said morosely. ''Why'd I ever open my mouth?''

''Good question,'' Kyle said.

Hollan didn't say anything for a minute, but then he gave a shrug in defeat. ''You know, Kyle, Jackie won't let up. She'll make my life miserable until you find us the perfect honeymoon. And she'll make your life miserable, too—because I'll be forced to hound you, never letting up until the job's done. So you and I really have no choice in the matter. Our hands are tied…. Women.''

Kyle leaned back in his chair. Hollan's newfound lack of logical thought process—blaming a whole gender for the mismanagement of his romantic concerns— was ridiculous. But one thing was clear. There really was going to be no peace until this honeymoon issue was resolved.

''At least I get to spend time with that sister of Jackie's,'' Kyle said.

''No kidding. You like her, don't you?''

''I like her, all right.'' Kyle felt that stirring of regret all over again. Spending time with Toni was a lot like his career crisis. It just made him more and more aware of the emptiness in his life…the emptiness he needed to fill, but didn't know how.

The problem was, he was trying to fill it with Toni. He wanted to be around her.

Too bad she didn't feel the same way.

# CHAPTER NINE

IN TONI'S OPINION, a house should be full of light—lots of windows, open wide to the sunshine. Certainly it should not be like the Martin home...musty, with the curtains pulled tight, the rooms small and claustrophobic.

Toni walked back and forth across the living room, her footsteps muffled by a shag carpet. Mr. and Mrs. Martin were staying with relatives. According to Mrs. Martin, neither she nor her husband could bear to be in the house where their grandchild had been killed. And, with their daughter in jail, they saw no reason to maintain even the semblance of a family. Mrs. Martin had loaned a key to Toni, but refused to come here herself today. Toni supposed that was all for the best. She wanted to get a feel for Sarah Martin's home on her own, no distractions or interruptions.

Toni paused at the spot where the little boy's body had been found—in front of a low veneer coffee table. According to the coroner's report, the child had suffered head injuries brought on by severe shaking. And, according to the police report, eighteen-year-old Sarah

Martin had been sitting beside her child's body when the officers first arrived. She hadn't been holding her son, hadn't been touching him in any way, hadn't been sobbing in grief or remorse. She had seemed completely detached from the situation.

Toni went down a cramped little hallway and looked in the first door on the right. She saw a bedroom with a carefully matched set of furniture—bureau, headboard, nightstands all finished a too-glossy brown. This was undoubtedly where Mr. and Mrs. Martin slept. There wasn't much character to the room. It was too neat, too sterile. Toni stood in the doorway and wondered about the couple who had spent night after night in this room. Despite profuse expressions of concern about their daughter, they hadn't attempted to raise bail for her. They thought being in custody might be the best thing for Sarah right now—the best thing for the family.

Toni reviewed the facts she knew about the Martins. Sarah's biological father had died when she was only three years old. When she was eight, her mother had remarried. Her stepfather had legally adopted her shortly thereafter. He worked as a hotel manager; Mrs. Martin worked in an insurance office. Mrs. Martin had confided to Toni that she'd always hoped her daughter would go to college. It had been a great disappointment when Sarah had become pregnant, and had not even finished high school. But both Mr. and Mrs. Martin—according to Mrs. Martin—had been overjoyed at the birth of their grandson. They had seen him as new hope for the family…and now he was gone.

Toni went down the hall and opened the door at the very end. She stepped over the threshold, feeling as if she had just entered the room of a very young girl. The bed was canopied, with a ruffled skirt. Several stuffed animals crowded atop a chest of drawers. Most of them looked well-used, well-loved. Toni picked up a small music box from a shelf and opened it. The tune that played was an outdated love song, and it sounded thin on the air. It also sounded melancholy.

On another shelf was a photograph in an ivory frame. It showed Sarah Martin and a boy, outfitted in prom clothes. Sarah looked very pretty, but there was still an aura of severity about her—a sense that she was not accustomed to feminine indulgences. She stood awkwardly in her lace and velvet dress, and she stared unsmiling into the camera. There was a peculiar blankness on her face, as if she defied anyone to read her true thoughts. The boy standing beside her looked earnest, and rather uncomfortable in his tuxedo. He wasn't touching Sarah as he, too, gazed into the camera. His expression was slightly startled, as if he hadn't expected a photo to be taken.

Toni gazed at the picture for a very long while, wondering if this could be Richard—the father of Sarah's baby. It seemed impossible that such a young,

unformed couple could produce a child. But Sarah
Martin had given birth to a baby boy when she was
only sixteen.

At last Toni set the photograph down and glanced
around the room again. The space was cramped, because of the extra furniture: a crib, a changing table,
a playpen folded and propped against the wall. The
crib had been stripped of sheets and blankets, and it
looked too bare. Toni settled down in a plain, sturdy
rocker beside the crib. She could imagine Sarah Martin
sitting here, rocking her child to sleep. Somehow she
could imagine that very well.

Toni sat and rocked, thinking about Sarah. It was
quite some time before she stood and went to the door
of the room. She glanced around again, taking note of
every detail. And then, quietly, she shut the door.

LATER THAT EVENING, when Toni let herself into her
parents' house, she was grateful for the welcoming
atmosphere that greeted her. She picked up Genevieve
and carried her to the kitchen.

"Mom, you here?"

"Mom's doing parents' night at school. Dad's still
at the bank. It's just me," Jackie announced as she sat
at the kitchen table, sipping a glass of milk. Toni de-
posited Genevieve on her blanket.

"How'd you get here?" she asked. Jackie had never
owned a car in the city.

"Hollan," Jackie muttered now. "Dear, *attentive* Hollan dropped me off."

Toni had the sinking sensation that Jackie and Hollan had argued again. Nonetheless, after the bleakness she'd encountered at the Martin house, she was glad to see her sister.

"How's my future niece or nephew?" she asked.

"The doctor says mother and baby are both doing fine." Jackie stared morosely at her glass of milk.

Toni thought about the empty crib in Sarah Martin's room. "Jackie," she said. "I'm glad you're having this baby. Awfully glad."

Jackie gave her a glance of surprise. "Really...I thought you saw it as one more of my stupid mistakes. *Hollan* sees it as a mistake."

Toni opened the fridge and took out a can of soda. She knew she shouldn't get more involved in Jackie's problems with Hollan. But Jackie looked so forlorn right now. Toni popped the lid on her soda and sat down across from her sister.

"What's wrong?" she asked.

"Everything! Take your pick. Hollan's making a big fuss about the napkins I chose for the reception. He says he doesn't understand why anyone would want to put a *love* poem on napkins. And he hates the caterer I picked. Says we can't possibly serve tofu rolls...every single decision I make, Hollan objects to it."

Toni took a good drink of her soda. "Jackie, listen to yourself. You keep talking about things *you* chose…decisions *you* made. Maybe Hollan just wants to be part of the wedding from the beginning."

"You don't get it," Jackie said. "I've tried to involve him in everything right from the start. Should we have a garden reception or an indoor buffet? Should we have the peach tablecloths, or the lilac? Every time I try for his input, he doesn't want to discuss it. So of course I have to go ahead and make the decision myself—and *then* he complains. *Then* he has all kinds of objections."

"Sounds like delay tactics to me," Toni said. "Jackie, according to Kyle, Hollan loves you buckets. Problem is, he's scared. Marriage, parenthood—the whole deal."

"Don't you think I'm scared, too?" Jackie blurted out. "It's all so confusing! Sometimes the thought of this baby makes me want to jump up and down with excitement. And other times…I ask myself how I can *possibly* be a mom. I planned to wait another five years, at least. I planned to get my career solidified first. None of this is part of the *plan*."

"Jackie…have you told Hollan any of this? It might make him feel better to know you're scared, too."

"I shouldn't have to tell him," Jackie muttered. "He should know what I need. Isn't that what love's all about?"

"He's not a mind reader, no matter how much he loves you. Just tell him how you're feeling. Let him in on it. He might surprise you."

Jackie pushed away her glass of milk. "What do *you* know about it?" she asked crabbily. "You've never been in love before—except with Greg, and he was an ass."

Old wounds began to smart. "If he was such an ass," Toni said, "then why did you flirt with him all the time?"

"Don't be absurd. I never flirted with Greg—"

"All the time, Jackie. What'd you want to do, steal my fiancé? You couldn't stand the thought that one man out there might actually prefer *me* to you? It wasn't enough that you had every other male at your feet?" Toni hated what she was saying, hated the way it spilled out, but she couldn't seem to stop herself.

Jackie stared at her, tight-lipped. "It wasn't like that. I could tell from the beginning Greg was a jerk— that he wasn't good enough for you. Believe me, I'd dated enough jerks to recognize one when I saw one."

"So you *flirted* with him—"

"Yes, all right, I did. I wanted to show you that any guy who flirted back the way he did couldn't be right for you—"

"Jackie, sometimes your logic astounds me."

"I was right about him," Jackie said stubbornly. "When you found out he was sleeping with that woman, it may have been a big shock to you, but not to *me*. I knew he'd end up doing something like that. I needed some way to let you know—"

"Stop," Toni said. "Please just stop."

Jackie sighed. "I know you think I'm self-centered and selfish, and all the rest of it. But I only want what's best for you, Toni. Do you think if you went out with some guy who's worth anything—some guy like Kyle Brennan—I'd flirt with *him?* No, of course I wouldn't.''

Toni propped her elbows on the table and wearily rested her head in her hands. Just as suddenly as they had come, the hurt and anger had drained out of her. "Like I say, Jackie…your logic escapes me."

"I've never so much as batted an eyelid at Kyle. And it's not just because after falling in love with Hollan I couldn't possibly flirt with *anyone*. It's because Kyle is…a man of quality. That's the only term for him. He might actually deserve you."

"How on earth did we get on the subject of Kyle Brennan?"

"Speaking of Kyle, how's the honeymoon search going?"

Toni groaned. "Please don't bring that up."

"Toni, Hollan and I are getting married in a matter of weeks. We need a honeymoon."

Toni thought about the trip she and Kyle had made to Honeymoon Ranch.

"You're blushing," said Jackie.

Toni put her hands to her face. "It's a little warm in here, that's all."

"The temperature is fine. Toni, please tell me what's going on."

"What's going on is…it's idiotic to have someone else pick your honeymoon."

"Don't I know it," Jackie said. "At first I couldn't believe it when Hollan came up with the idea."

Toni gave her sister a look of disbelief. "Jackie, the words were no sooner out his mouth before you latched on to them."

"A matter of expediency," Jackie said. "These are extraordinary circumstances. Hollan and I simply can't agree on a honeymoon. He refuses to compromise—won't give an inch."

"And you, I suppose, you're willing to compromise no end."

"I'm willing to give what's necessary," Jackie said.

"Right," Toni muttered. "That's why you've told Hollan you can only go on a three-day honeymoon."

"Toni, do you realize what a vulnerable position I'm in at work? I could be replaced just like that. I can't give them even a *chance* to think about it."

Toni shook her head. "If that's the case—and I doubt it is—what will you do when the baby comes?"

"I can't possibly think that far ahead," Jackie said rigidly. "All I know is that Hollan and I need a honeymoon. Something special…something wonderful…something to show us we're meant to be together, after all.''

This crazy situation was getting worse by the minute. "You don't ask for much, do you?" Toni said. "Only perfection, in three days. But Jackie, if you and Hollan are having so much trouble, why don't you just delay the wedding? Work things out first.''

"Maybe I could have done that before the baby. But things are different now. My child has to be welcomed into a home with two parents. That's the way things are supposed to be.''

"Plenty of women are single parents," Toni argued. "They manage—"

"My child will have *two* parents, living in the same home. That's the way we were raised, and that's how it has to be.''

Toni could tell she wasn't getting through to her sister. It was true that the two of them had been raised in an ideal situation. But you couldn't always turn reality into the ideal.

"I don't see why both Kyle and I have to choose the honeymoon," Toni said. "I say let Kyle do it on his own. He has good taste—that's one thing I know about him.''

"You can't be serious," Jackie said. "You both have to do it. We need one person from each camp.''

"Each camp," Toni echoed. "Jackie, listen to yourself. One minute you want the perfect little family, and the next you talk like you and Hollan are at war.''

"I know it's crazy," Jackie said. "I know Hollan and I should be able to stop bickering long enough to pick our own damn honeymoon. I know we shouldn't have a power struggle over every little thing. I know we shouldn't argue, and make up, and argue again, all in the space of ten minutes. I know we should be kind and giving and wise and every other virtue you've ever heard of. I know all those things, Toni! But you know what else I know? I know that if I ever lose Hollan, I'll *die.* So, yes, I cling to the idea that you and Kyle will find us the perfect honeymoon. A little patch of paradise somewhere, a place where Hollan and I might actually stop all the fighting and all the being scared...and maybe just love each other..."

A tall order, indeed. An impossible one, in fact. Yet Jackie sounded so wistful, so sad. Toni gazed at her sister, and no longer had the heart to argue.

The front door opened and closed. A few seconds later, Marianne Shaw came into the kitchen.

"Both my girls," she said. "How wonderful."

"Mom," Jackie said plaintively. She stood and went to Marianne for a hug.

"Hey, kiddo, it'll be all right," Marianne said, patting her youngest daughter on the back. Toni watched the two of them. This was a familiar scenario—Marianne engulfed by Jackie's life, Jackie's woes. Right now, Toni didn't mind. She and her mother shared a glance, and she knew they were both thinking the same thing: they wanted Jackie to be happy.

With all the comforting maternal murmurings Toni remembered from her childhood, Marianne got Jackie seated again.

"You're drinking milk—good," said Marianne. "No, honey, don't worry a bit about gaining weight already. I saw your five-thirty broadcast today, and you looked fantastic."

In the midst of her mother's efforts to soothe Jackie, Toni noticed the distracted look in Marianne's eyes, the little tension lines that seemed to be etching deeper into her forehead.

"Mom," Toni said at last, "I came over tonight because I'm worried about you."

"Me? Don't be silly—"

"I'm worried about you and Dad."

Jackie lifted her head and glanced in consternation from her mother to her sister.

"What's this about Mom and Dad?"

"Nothing, dear," said Marianne. "There's no reason to concern yourself. You have enough problems of your own—"

"Jackie probably wants to know what's going on with her own parents," Toni said.

"Yes," Jackie said. "I do. Mom, you always try to

protect me. But if you're having troubles, I'd darn well like to know about them."

Marianne put up both her hands. "All right, all right, my daughters win. Here's the long and short of it. Your dad wants to retire immediately and go off jaunting around the world. He wants me to quit my job, toss everything else aside and go with him. Well, I love my job…and I have plans…plans of my own. I don't want to tear my life up by the roots. But your dad…your dad just won't listen."

"Oh, Lord," Jackie said. "He sounds just like Hollan."

"I've tried everything," Marianne said. "Possible alternatives, reasoned negotiation on all points, and still he won't listen." She was beginning to sound desperate. "So you know what I did, girls? I loaned all our luggage to your cousin Millie. I canceled the auto club. I fired our travel agent. And I hid all your dad's trip folders from A to Z. He'll never find his brochures on Amsterdam or Zanzibar, and everything in between."

Jackie looked at Toni. "This is bad," she said. "You told me that Hollan and I sound like we're at war. But this is even worse. With Mom and Dad, it's…*guerilla* warfare!"

NEXT AFTERNOON, Toni arrived at Heritage City's small airpark. She got out of her car and waited not far from the runway. Glancing at her watch, she saw that she was right on time. If only she knew why she was here.

Kyle had been very mysterious over the phone. He'd simply asked her to meet him at this place—wouldn't say what it was about. She'd been half tempted to tell him no. Hadn't he disrupted her life enough already?

Apparently not. Because here she was, waiting for him, unable to deny a pleasant sense of anticipation. She was actually looking forward to seeing the man.

A little green-and-white plane appeared in the sky. Toni watched as it drew closer, descending to the runway and coming to a stop near where she stood. It was a small seaplane, with a pontoon under each wing and a rounded belly. One of the doors cranked open and a few seconds later out climbed Kyle Brennan. He waved when he saw her. She waved back, foolishly glad to see him. When he reached her side, she tried to disguise her pleasure.

"Well," she said, "so flying is one of your talents."

He grinned. "Actually, I'm still working on my pilot's license. My friend Steve flew me down from San Francisco."

Toni had already noticed the other man in the cockpit. Her gaze, however, focused on Kyle. This was the first time she'd ever seen him in shorts. They were the sturdy variety, made of canvas with cargo pockets. Toni found that she was staring at Kyle's well-shaped, muscular legs. She saw some attractive freckles on his knees.

"Are you ready?" he asked.

"Every time you say that, I start to worry."

"You've escaped your office for the day, haven't you?" he went on.

"Yes," she said reluctantly. "But I have some files to work on at home tonight. Which means I can't take long, whatever you have in mind—"

"Business, Antonia. Honeymoon business."

"Oh, well, why didn't you say so in the first place?" she grumbled. "When it comes to honeymoons, I have a list of places to check out." She went to her car, rummaged through her briefcase and produced the aforementioned list. "I think we can be efficient about it. We'll make a preliminary phone call to each location and ask very specific questions. If the location passes this initial test, we'll move on to the next step—"

"Toni...no list. No preliminaries. Not today. Today we use my method."

"Didn't we use your method last time?" she asked. "Something about just going by how a place makes you feel..."

"Exactly." He took her hand and drew her toward

the plane. "My friend Steve is going to fly us someplace. And we're going to see how it makes us feel."

"Already I don't have a good feeling about this,"
she said. But, before she knew it, she was on the plane
with Kyle. And, together, they were leaving Heritage
City far behind.

# CHAPTER TEN

SOARING WITH Kyle Brennan was exhilarating. High above the California coast, Toni felt buoyant, light-hearted. It was as if, the moment they'd taken off from the runway, she'd left ordinary, day-to-day concerns behind. But wasn't this how Kyle always made her feel?

The sky was a brilliant blue, and so was the Pacific stretching out far below. Kyle's friend flew for a while, but then Kyle himself took the controls. He handled the plane just as effortlessly and gracefully as he did everything else. Toni wondered if there was *any-thing* he did not do well.

"Too good to be true," she muttered under her breath.

"What was that?" Kyle asked.

"Just admiring the scenery." She'd moved up into the front beside Kyle, and Steve had taken the rear seat. Steve was Kyle's flying instructor, a man of about forty-five who, with a little encouragement from Kyle, had already proudly shown Toni pictures of his three kids. As always, Kyle had demonstrated a knack for drawing those around him easily into conversation. Without trying too hard, he made sure that no one got left out. Yet another talent…definitely a man too good to be true.

"I don't suppose you'll tell me where we're headed," Toni said.

"It's a surprise, Antonia."

She glanced back at Steve. "Don't suppose you'll spill the beans."

"I'm sworn to secrecy."

It seemed Toni really did have no choice other than to admire the sparkle of ocean and the sweep of coastline below. They flew south for a while, but Toni lost track of how long. Time didn't seem very important, and she didn't even glance at her watch.

A small island appeared in the expanse of water. "Steve," Kyle said, "you'd better take over. I haven't done any water landings yet."

Toni was glad to hear there was at least one thing Kyle didn't do perfectly. But this only highlighted another good quality about him: his ability to admit he wasn't perfect.

"There's no winning," Toni muttered.

"What was that, Antonia?" Kyle asked.

She gave him a sardonic glance. "Still just admiring the view."

The two men exchanged places, and now the plane descended near the island. It landed in the water with somewhat unwieldy grace, like a duck splashing into a pond. Riding the ocean, the little plane rocked with the waves as they taxied over beside a pier. Kyle climbed out first, then helped Toni scramble onto the pier. Steve waved goodbye.

"Wait—you're not staying?" Toni asked him.

"Have to get back. It's just you and Kyle."

Toni had been afraid of that. She turned to glare at Kyle. But one look at the damn grin on his face told her any argument would be futile. She watched as the plane took off again, banking to head back north, leaving her alone with Kyle. He'd brought a knapsack with him from the plane, and now he swung it over his shoulder. Toni had her briefcase. She turned, ready to follow him along the dock, but then she stood still at what she saw.

"Oh my," she breathed.

"What do you think?" Kyle asked.

"It's like…it's like paradise," she said simply.

They were facing a deep cove, the sands shimmering golden white in the late-afternoon sun. Waves lapped against the shore. And, presiding on a rocky outcrop above the beach, was one of the loveliest structures Toni had ever seen: a rambling mansion in weathered gray shingle, with Queen Anne turrets and gabled dormers and wraparound porches.

"Oh my," she said again.

"I agree," said Kyle. He took her hand, and they

walked the rest of the way up the pier. "Careful," he said. Some of the boards had warped and the going was uneven. But Toni didn't mind. She was entranced by the island.

"What is this place?" she murmured. "Have we stepped back in time somehow…"

"Makes you wish for that, doesn't it? This used to be a pretty exclusive resort. Built in 1890, I'm told. Did pretty well until World War I, but then the original owner couldn't keep it up. It's been through several hands since then."

They crossed the sand and climbed a long flight of wooden steps leading up to the mansion, arriving on one of the porches. Toni walked all along its length, the floorboards giving a satisfying creak now and then. She peered through a dusty window.

"I wish we could go inside," she said.

"Your wish is my command," Kyle said, producing a large old-fashioned key from one of his pockets.

"There's obviously more to this than you're telling," she said. "How did you find out about this place?"

"All in good time," he said.

"Do you have to be so mysterious?" she asked.

"Just trust me, Toni. This could be the perfect honeymoon location." He opened one of the doors for her. She stepped over the threshold, and discovered that the place was as lovely inside as out. A spacious

# Play **TIC-TAC-TOE** and get **FREE GIFTS!**

## HOW TO PLAY:

1. Play the tic-tac-toe scratch-off game at the right for your FREE BOOKS and FREE GIFT!

2. Send back this card and you'll receive TWO brand-new Harlequin Superromance® novels. These books have a cover price of $4.25 each, but they are yours to keep absolutely free.

3. There's no catch. You're under no obligation to buy anything. We charge nothing — ZERO — for your first shipment. And you don't have to make any minimum number of purchases — not even one!

4. The fact is, thousands of readers enjoy receiving books by mail from the Harlequin Reader Service® months before they're available in stores. They like the convenience of home delivery, and they love our discount prices!

5. We hope that after receiving your free books you'll want to remain a subscriber. But the choice is yours — to continue or cancel, any time at all! So why not take us up on our invitation, with no risk of any kind. You'll be glad you did!

YOURS **FREE**

A FABULOUS **MYSTERY GIFT!**

We can't tell you what it is...
but we're sure you'll like it!

**A FREE GIFT** –
just for playing
**TIC-TAC-TOE!**

**DETACH AND MAIL CARD TODAY!**

**First**, scratch the gold boxes on the tic-tac-toe board. Then remove the "X" sticker from the front and affix it so that you get three X's in a row. This means you can get **TWO FREE** Harlequin Superromance® novels and a **FREE MYSTERY GIFT!**

**PLAY TIC-TAC-TOE**

**YES!** Please send me all the gifts for which I qualify. I understand that I am under no obligation to purchase any books, as explained on the back of this card.

(U-H-SR-08/98)

**134 HDL CH52**

Name
(PLEASE PRINT CLEARLY)

Address _____ Apt.#

City _____ State _____ Zip _____

# The Harlequin Reader Service® — Here's how it works:

Accepting free books places you under no obligation to buy anything. You may keep the books and gift and return the shipping statement marked "cancel." If you do not cancel, about a month later we'll send you 4 additional novels and bill you just $3.57 each, plus 25¢ delivery per book and applicable sales tax, if any.* That's the complete price — and compared to cover prices of $4.25 each — quite a bargain! You may cancel at any time, but if you choose to continue, every month we'll send you 4 more books, which you may either purchase at the discount price...or return to us and cancel your subscription.

*Terms and prices subject to change without notice. Sales tax applicable in N.Y.

If offer card is missing write to: Harlequin Reader Service, 3010 Walden Ave., P.O. Box 1867, Buffalo NY 14240-1867

## BUSINESS REPLY MAIL
FIRST-CLASS MAIL    PERMIT NO. 717    BUFFALO, NY

POSTAGE WILL BE PAID BY ADDRESSEE

HARLEQUIN READER SERVICE
3010 WALDEN AVE
PO BOX 1867
BUFFALO NY 14240-9952

NO POSTAGE
NECESSARY
IF MAILED
IN THE
UNITED STATES

hall with a center chimney, slate floors…an octagonal room with French windows…another room in walnut wainscoting…best of all, a turret room, snugly round with high ceilings, making Toni feel as if she were in a lighthouse. And over everything lay a film of dust, a patina of nostalgia. Sand had blown in through the cracks, sun-bleached sheets draped the few remaining pieces of furniture, paint had faded to soft, muted shades.

"With a little bit of work," Kyle said, "this could be a honeymoon spot, all right."

"Yes, it could," Toni said dreamily. "Here's what I'd do. I'd cart a bunch of provisions over from the mainland, and then I'd just hole up here with my new husband. We'd pitch a sleeping bag in one of the rooms. The morning sun coming through the windows would wake us up, and we'd spend every day on the beach…" Her voice trailed off when she saw the thoughtful way Kyle was watching her. "A hypothetical situation," she added.

"Right. Since you don't believe in husbands, you can't very well have a honeymoon."

"The point is, would Jackie and Hollan like to spend their honeymoon here?"

Kyle gave her another thoughtful glance, but he answered her question. "Hollan would do just fine. He could bring along his scuba gear."

"I'm not so sure about Jackie. Her idea of roughing

it is having to use a rotary phone to dial room service.''

"Let's not write off the place just yet," Kyle said.

"Okay, fess up," she told him. "What's really going on here? This island isn't exactly on any of the tourist maps, but you seem to know more about it than you're letting on. Plus, you have a key. What gives?''

"I'll tell you—but not on an empty stomach.'' He led the way back outside and sat down on the top step of the beach stairs. Toni settled beside him as he produced several items from his knapsack: cranberry juice, apple juice, two candy bars, a packet of trail mix, a packet of crackers.

"Another picnic,'' Toni said.

"Afraid not. It's only official when I have Aunt Eileen's basket.''

Toni began eating a candy bar savoring the rich chocolate.

"Here's how it is,'' said Kyle. "A couple of years ago, Hollan and I designed an office complex for a guy by the name of Russell Parker. Seems Russ bought this entire island not too long ago. And when he heard Hollan needed a honeymoon, he suggested we check the place out.''

Toni finished her chocolate, and Kyle handed her the other one.

"I shouldn't,'' she said.

"Why not?"

She tore open the wrapper. "I doubt your Mr. Parker bought this island just so it could be a honeymoon hideaway."

"Actually, that's not so far from the truth. Russ wants this place to become a resort again. And he wants me to oversee the planning and design phase."

"Wow," Toni said.

"Maybe 'wow.' Part of me doesn't like the fact that this isolation would change. Russ wants to add new buildings—he's almost thinking a small town. Told me he'd keep the spirit of the original resort, but still…I wonder if he can pull it off."

"It'll be tough," Toni agreed. Then a thought struck her. "Kyle—your friend Russ wouldn't try to tear down this building, would he?"

"No, he's already talked about renovating it, so it could be the centerpiece of the new resort."

"That's great. Are you going to consider the job?"

"I'm thinking about it," Kyle said, as if to himself. "Talk about a whole new direction in my career…" He stood and walked along the porch, then leaned against the railing to gaze out toward the ocean. Toni went to stand next to him.

"Tell me what you're thinking."

"The job has its good points. It would be a new challenge, unlike anything I've ever done before. This island is someplace special—you and I both can see that. The idea would be to complement the surroundings. It would have to be done just right. Definitely a challenge.''

Toni listened to the enthusiasm in his voice. It was the way he'd sounded when he'd been designing a house for *her*. But that project was over with. A sense of loss came over her again. She tried to tell herself it was for the best, but still…

''Heck, maybe you should do it,'' she said. ''Maybe you should take on this island.''

''Maybe. It'd be a big job, and I'd have to make sure Russ and I see eye to eye.'' He paused. ''I asked Hollan if he'd want to do this project with me, but it's just not the kind of work that interests him. Makes me realize more than ever that it's time to move on from our partnership. Hollan knows it—I know it.''

''You're still friends,'' Toni said.

''Yep. We just won't be partners anymore.''

''I see,'' Toni remarked. ''Now let's do some more exploring. I want to see some more of the island.''

AN HOUR OR SO LATER, they'd done a whole lot of exploring. The island wasn't very large, and since no one was living on it at the moment, they had it all to themselves. Much of the terrain was rugged and windswept, possessing an isolated grandeur. There were also nooks and crannies where palms and other lush greenery flourished. Best of all, however, were the small coves and inlets here and there, hidden places where the ocean beckoned.

"Damn," Toni said at last. "Wish I'd brought my swimsuit."

"You don't need one," Kyle said. "Toss off your clothes and jump in."

She frowned at him.

"Toni," he said. "Nothing's going to happen."

"Nothing…"

"You've made pretty sure I'd get the message. You don't want anything to happen, so it won't."

"Fine," she said, wondering why she felt so dissatisfied. But they'd reached one particularly inviting stretch of beach, and Toni could no longer resist. Going off a short distance from Kyle, she slipped off her loafers and socks. After a second's hesitation, she unzipped her pants and chucked those, too. Her cotton shirt came down to the tops of her thighs, and she supposed that would do. She waded out into the surf.

The water temperature was just right, cool as it lapped against her legs. She waded out farther, and now the water dampened her shirt. She forgot all inhibitions as she splashed onto her back, allowing a wave to carry her. From this distance, she watched as Kyle took off his hiking boots and socks. Next came his shirt, the afternoon sun glinting on the reddish hair across his chest. And then, without any self-consciousness whatsoever, off came his shorts. Staring at him, Toni almost went under when another wave came along.

Clad in nothing but a pair of black briefs, Kyle swam out to join her. Together they paddled farther out. The coolness of the water and the warmth of the sun had an intoxicating effect.

"I don't think I ever want to go back," Toni said impulsively. "Forget the mainland. Forget responsibilities and obligations."

"So we'll stay on the island and live off candy bars."

"At night we'll make a fire on the beach and toast marshmallows," she said.

"No alarm clocks. No phones. No schedules."

"We'd be bored in about twenty-four hours, wouldn't we?" Toni asked.

"Nah...give it at least two weeks."

Personally, Toni thought it would take at least a month. She and Kyle swam some more, letting the waves have their way, but as the sun began dipping toward later afternoon, they headed for shore. As Toni emerged from the water, her wet shirt clinging to her, she began to shiver a little.

"You should have taken that off," Kyle said. "No need for false modesty around me." Matter-of-factly, he unbuttoned her shirt and drew it away from her. She sat down in the sand, feeling much too exposed in her bra and underwear. Kyle took his own shirt and put it around her.

"Much better," she said.

Kyle turned away for a minute to retrieve his shorts. Toni had a tantalizing view of a very well-shaped male posterior in those wet briefs. Then on went his shorts, and he turned around again. Quickly she tried to act mesmerized by the ocean.

"Forget it," he said. "You've been caught."

"Okay, so I looked," she said grouchily.

He stretched out in the sand beside her. "Why is it," he said, "that guys pride themselves on taking a look every chance they get, but women try to pretend they never take a look?"

"Just one of those puzzling questions that can't be answered," Toni said.

He put his hands behind his head and closed his eyes. Which left Toni with the perfect opportunity to take a long look. That swirl of russet hair on his chest, those muscles defining his forearms...even his feet were sexy.

Toni allowed her gaze to drift over Kyle's body until it focused on his mouth. Only gradually did she realize that she wasn't shivering anymore. The soft material of Kyle's shirt had warmed her. Without stopping to think, she lay on the sand beside him. She continued gazing at his mouth. And then, still without any heed to reason at all, she leaned over him and brushed her lips against his.

He reached a hand up, buried it in her damp hair. But he did not deepen the contact between them. He seemed to be waiting for her to lead the way. Experimentally, she probed her tongue over his lips. Still no response. Enticed, intrigued, she shifted her weight until she was half leaning against him. Again she probed with the tip of her tongue. She felt his lips curve into a smile beneath hers.

They kissed for a long moment, the ocean breeze drifting over them. And then Kyle took command, turning her gently until his shirt fell away from her. He kissed her, and he looked at her. He made no pretense.

"You're beautiful, Toni."

The flimsy lace of her bra afforded no protection from his gaze. She wished she could cross her arms in front of her.

"I'm average," she said.

"Average...no. Beautiful." He bent his head and kissed her again. She could lose herself in his arms, his touch. Any remnant of chill vanished in the heat of his caress. Toni put her arms around him, brought him closer...

But this time he was the one who ended the kiss. He sat up. "We have to leave," he said.

"What...?"

"A boat's coming to pick us up in about five minutes."

"Oh, Lord." Toni couldn't believe she was sprawled here in nothing but her skivvies, still warmed by Kyle Brennan's touch. She scrambled to her feet, grabbed her slacks and pulled them on. Her own shirt was still too wet, so she put on Kyle's. Never mind that it hung loose around her. Next her socks and shoes. Never mind the sand between her toes.

Kyle took a more leisurely time putting on his socks and boots. He gathered up her damp shirt. She didn't wait for him, but went hurrying on down the beach.

"Running away again," he said when he caught up to her.

"So far I've only seen one dock on this island. Unless you tell me otherwise, that's where I'm headed."

"That's where they're picking us up, all right," he said. "But you're still running away from me."

"I just can't believe I did it again," she muttered. "Got myself into a compromising position with you...I really feel stupid."

"It wasn't so compromising," he said. "Even without the boat coming, I wouldn't have let things go any further."

"*You* wouldn't let..." She glanced at him. "You think you were that much in charge of the situation?"

"Had to be, Antonia. Anything more happens, and you give me hell for it."

She heard the familiar laughter skimming his voice.

"Great," she said. "So *you* wouldn't regret... anything more happening."

He took her hand. "Toni, if we ever made love, there's no possible way I could regret it."

She moved her fingers in his. "You make it sound like no more of an indulgence than—than eating a candy bar."

"It would be a lot better than that," he said solemnly. "I promise."

Toni found it infuriating that she couldn't tell whether he was serious or whether he was joking. Maybe she'd never know. But that boat was coming, and she had to get herself into some semblance of dignity. They arrived back at the cove beside the big house. Toni had left her briefcase next to Kyle's knapsack at the bottom of the beach steps. It was a relief to open the briefcase and take out the accoutrements that bespoke order and control: her brush and comb, her lip gloss, her red scarf. She organized her damp hair, using the scarf to hold it off her face.

"I like you that way," Kyle told her. "The scarf says you're ready for the unexpected."

"I thought it said exactly the opposite." She buckled the briefcase down tight, then walked out onto the pier.

"Careful," Kyle told her as he came along beside her. "This thing's as old as the house."

"I'll manage," Toni said. Indeed, she felt in control again. Except for the small fact that she was still wearing Kyle's shirt, she was almost back to normal. She sat down at the very edge of the pier, her legs dangling over the water. Kyle sat beside her.

"They should be coming for us just about now," he said. "Russ arranged for a charter, and he'll have a car waiting for us, too."

"Good," Toni said.

"I don't know...I kinda hate to leave."

She felt the same way, but she wasn't about to admit it.

They waited. No boat came. Toni glanced at her watch. They waited some more. No boat.

"Kyle..."

"Should've been here by now." He didn't seem worried.

"Maybe we ought to call and find out what the holdup is."

Obligingly, he took his cell phone out of the knapsack. He punched in a number, listened for a few seconds. "No dice. Definitely out of range."

"For goodness' sake, let's try mine." She unbuckled her briefcase, pulled out her own phone.

No dice.

"Maybe the boat's just late," Toni said.

They waited some more. And waited. Afternoon had mellowed toward evening.

"It can't be," Toni said.

"Afraid so. We might just be stranded, Antonia."

She stared at him in dismay. "Not again."

They waited some more. No boat. And Toni could no longer deny the truth. First the wine country, and now an enchanted island.

She kept getting stuck with Kyle in the most romantic places.

# CHAPTER ELEVEN

DUSK HAD FALLEN upon the gray-shingle mansion. As Toni walked through the place, shadows evoked more than ever the sense of a long-ago time. In one room she lifted a corner of a sheet, saw an upright piano hidden underneath. Toni pressed one of the keys, and a minor note sounded on the air.

"Found some matches," Kyle said as he entered the room. "Ancient, but maybe they'll still work." He came over next to the piano.

"If you tell me you play, on top of everything else you do, I'm leaving," Toni said. It was an empty threat, since the boat definitely had not appeared.

"You didn't take piano lessons when you were a kid?" he asked.

"Violin," she said. "I was so lousy at it my parents finally let me quit just so they could have some peace."

"I played clarinet for a year. Although *played* might not be the right word. Drove my sisters crazy, more like it."

"I don't believe it," she said. "You're not bad at

anything, Kyle.'' She allowed the sheet to drape back over the piano.

''Right now I'm bad at figuring out what to do with my life,'' he said.

''There's something to be said for taking one day at a time,'' Toni murmured. On the island, time didn't seem important; at this moment, it didn't seem necessary to think about the future.

''I'd say we've been through the entire place,'' Kyle said. ''Rounded up all the supplies we're likely to.''

Toni examined her own cache. Upstairs she'd found two yellowed magazines dated 1957, a battery-run lantern with no batteries and a quilt in surprisingly good shape.

''The quilt should come in handy,'' she said, ''but the other stuff won't do us any good.''

''You never know—bring everything.'' He went across the hall to a room that had a stone fireplace. ''I found some wood in a shed out back—we'll be set in no time.'' Kyle proceeded to lay the wood on the hearth. Soon he had a cozy fire burning. Toni spread the quilt in front of the hearth and sat down crosslegged. She'd already given Kyle back his shirt, and she wore the light jacket he'd brought along in his knapsack. By now she felt toasty warm.

Kyle sat beside her, and handed her another candy bar.

''How many of these do you have?'' she asked.

He looked inside the knapsack. "Just enough for dinner," he said.

They ate the candy, the crackers and the trail mix. Kyle produced another cranberry juice, and they shared that, too. Toni glanced at Kyle, and saw the way the firelight flickered over his features, emphasizing the firm line of his jaw. He looked good by firelight. But when *didn't* he look good?

He picked up one of the magazines she'd found. "Told you this would come in handy," he said. "We can read about what was going on forty years ago."

"I already looked at some of the articles—they're hopeless. All about how to catch a man and how to make the perfect casserole once you've caught him."

"Nothing about how to catch a woman?"

"Hardly," Toni said.

"Guys worry about those things too, you know."

"Kyle, I seriously doubt you've ever had to worry about chasing any female. I'm sure they've flocked to you all your life."

"Hell, no," he said. "Lately, the only thing that happens is that Hollan sets me up. I have a bad experience, and then he sets me up again."

"You keep letting him do it," Toni said. "That says something."

"Yeah, says I have a hard time telling Hollan no."

"It says you're looking for a woman," Toni informed him.

He leaned back on his elbow and smiled lazily. "What if I've already found her? What if you're the woman, Antonia?"

She felt her heart beat a little faster. "Thank goodness we both know the answer to that. No way."

"How can you be so sure?" he asked. "Maybe I'm your destiny...not good old Dan Greene."

"I don't believe in destiny," she said. "Men and women just stumble around and make the most dreadful decisions about each other. No use blaming it on fate."

"You don't think it's fate we're here together...tonight?"

There was a huskiness in his voice that sent a quiver down her spine. She wrapped her arms around her knees and stared into the fire.

"Kyle, you're not telling me you planned this, are you?"

"No," he said regretfully. "Something tells me it's just a mix-up about the boat. But it would've been a damn good idea if I'd come up with it myself—getting you stranded here with me."

She wanted to avoid looking at him. But somehow, against her own will, she turned her head slowly and gazed at him. The fire cast a mysterious play of light and shadow over his face. As always, she never quite knew whether to take him seriously.

She stood. "I really did want to get some work done tonight," she said.

"Hey, you have your briefcase," he said. "I won't disturb you. I'll just sit here and read these magazines about the perfect casserole."

She gave him an exasperated glance.

He grinned. "Go ahead—work," he said.

She didn't think she'd get anything done, sitting in front of a fireplace with Kyle Brennan. "It's just the Martin case," she said. "It's on my mind more and more. Sarah Martin...she's on my mind." Toni went to a window, pressed her hand to the cold glass. It was so dark outside now that she couldn't see the ocean, could only hear the waves rolling against the beach. "This place really is enchanted," she murmured. "It makes you wonder...if everybody had a place like this, maybe all the bad things in the world wouldn't happen. If Sarah had ever had a place like this, instead of that mean little house where she grew up..."

"Do you think she's innocent?" Kyle asked quietly.

"I don't know...I honestly don't know. But I'm going to keep digging, that much is for sure. There's a whole lot she's not telling. And maybe a whole lot her parents aren't telling, either."

Kyle was the one who reached over, took her briefcase and placed it on the quilt. "Work, Toni," he said. "If it's what you need to do, go ahead."

She *was* itching to get at the files she'd brought—

past cases from the office archives that might give her some precedents for the Martin case. After only a second's hesitation, she sat down, cross-legged again, and opened her briefcase. She pulled out the files, as well as a notepad and a pen. Kyle was already leafing through one of the magazines. The fire gave just enough light to see by. Toni began work, jotting down notes as she examined each file.

It was oddly companionable, being with Kyle like this...together, yet occupied in separate pursuits. At one point, Kyle got up to stoke the fire, then asked her if she had some extra sheets of paper. She provided them, as well as a pencil. He began sketching something, his expression intent. Toni went on working, but her gaze returned to Kyle now and again. Yes...this was very companionable.

At last she set the files aside, surprised to find that her fingers were cramped from writing. She looked at Kyle. He'd assumed what appeared to be a favorite position, stretched out on his side, head propped in one hand. He continued to sketch, pages strewn around him. He seemed very involved in what he was doing, just as involved as Toni had been in her own work.

Finally he glanced up, too. "Done already?" he asked.

"I think we've been at this a couple of hours, at least," she said.

He straightened. "They say time flies when you're having fun."

"You did seem to be having fun, Kyle."

He shrugged. "Just some ideas for this place, if I decide to take on the job."

"Don't tell me," Toni said. "You were...inspired."

"Maybe I was, at that."

"So this inspiration thing—maybe it's not so elusive, after all. Maybe you can have it more often than you thought."

"Maybe," he acknowledged. He still seemed lost in his own thoughts, but then he stirred. "How about you—any inspiration?"

"Just a few ideas. Maybe some ammunition next time my boss tells me I have to plea this case out instead of taking it to court." She paused awkwardly. "Well, I guess we could catch some shut-eye. I don't know about you, but I'm getting tired."

He put his sketches aside, stretched out even farther and patted the quilt beside him.

"Kyle..."

"Relax, Toni. It's going to be a cold night even with the fire—that's all. Like I told you...nothing's going to happen."

He sounded maddeningly in control. But wasn't that what Toni wanted—to keep the night under control?

If only Kyle didn't cause such a contradictory mix of emotions inside her...

She lay down. He put his arm around her and tucked her next to him. "Body heat," he said. "That's all we're sharing."

Body heat...indeed.

THE FIRST LIGHT of dawn woke Toni. She was amazed that she'd slept at all. Lying in the arms of an incredibly handsome man just didn't seem conducive to restful sleep. But somehow she had managed it. As she opened her eyes, she realized that Kyle still had one arm flung over her. He was breathing deeply and evenly. The fire had banked down, and the morning was cool. But here, next to Kyle, she was warm.

She lay still, not wanting to wake him. But a thought was taking shape in her mind...an alarming, unexpected thought that was rapidly destroying any peace of mind she had. It came in the form of a question that repeated itself, over and over. *Was she falling in love with Kyle Brennan? Was she actually falling in love with the man?*

At last there was no choice. She had to move. As carefully as possible, she slipped away from him, reaching for her loafers. Then she tiptoed toward the door. When she glanced back at the quilt, she saw Kyle sitting up and yawning.

"Um, sorry I woke you," she said hurriedly. "I'm just going for a walk."

He began to rise.

"Alone, Kyle," she said. "I need to take a walk alone."

He didn't answer, just gave her a reflective look. She escaped outside, and went down the beach stairs. The sky was painted in streaks of rose and gold. Her feet left imprints in the damp sand as she walked along the surf. She wished that she could outdistance the question that had popped into her head. But it stayed with her, taunting her.

Was she falling in love with Kyle? Was she that reckless, that foolish?

Toni gave a small groan. It couldn't be possible. She couldn't let it happen! She couldn't bear to fall in love again…she couldn't bear to feel that vulnerable. Not ever again.

Nonetheless, the question remained. Spending the night in Kyle's arms—without so much as a hint of making love—somehow increased her turmoil. There had been an intimacy about the night, something that went beyond mere physical contact. It was as if they had shared something much deeper, something she didn't know how to put into words.

Toni walked back and forth along the shore, trying to order her emotions. Almost from the beginning she'd been thinking Kyle was a man too good to be true. Didn't he have *some* flaw she was overlooking? Some flaw she could get a handle on, something that would give her perspective…

She turned, and saw him coming down the beach stairs. As he drew closer, she noted the stubble of red beard along his jaw, the rumpled appearance of his hair. Why did those facts only add to his appeal?

"Don't even do it," she said as he came up to her. "Don't tell me that I'm running away from you."

"Aren't you?" he asked conversationally.

"I just wanted a little time to myself, so I could think."

"About me?" he asked, deadpan.

She gazed at him hard. And she saw it—the humor, glimmering just below the surface.

"You know, Kyle," she said, "I *have* been out here thinking about you. I've been trying to find some flaw in your character…and I've found it. You start to act as if there could be something serious between us, but then you back off by turning it into a joke. It's like you're hedging your bets. There's only one problem— this isn't Las Vegas and we're not gambling." She turned and walked away from him, feeling triumphant about her assessment.

As usual, he kept pace with her. "Don't be so ready to judge," he told her. "Maybe I *am* serious."

"Are you?" she asked skeptically. "Then tell me something, Kyle. Have you ever considered what being serious might really mean? No...let's go all the way here. Let's talk marriage. Have you ever thought about what it means to be married—I mean, really married?''

He didn't answer for quite some time, and she was sure she'd stumped him. But then he spoke.

''I thought about it last night,'' he said. ''When you and I were sitting in front of the fire, and we each had something to work on, something that engaged us and took all our attention. It occurred to me that marriage could be like that...a good marriage, anyway. Two people mature enough to have individual pursuits, individual personalities, but who find a common ground at the same time. Yeah, I thought about it.''

Toni fought the image he'd conjured. ''That was only one night we spent together, Kyle. Marriage is one day after the other—after the other. Even my mom and dad, after all the time they've been together, they're still having a difficult time getting it right. My mother's even resorting to sabotage these days. So you see, I just don't think it's all that easy.''

''I didn't say easy. Hell, Toni, nothing with you is easy. But maybe I keep coming around because I find you so damn fascinating anyway.'' He sounded disgruntled, and Toni gave him a sideways glance.

''Kyle, you're not asking me to marry you, are you?'' she asked dryly.

He didn't say anything, just looked back at her.

"By the way, that was me making a joke," she said. "You, of all people, should recognize a joke."

"Toni, what would you say if I told you I've considered the thought? Marriage...you and me."

She stared at him, speechless. Her heart had started to thump way too fast. She couldn't think of a word to say in response—not a single word. But just then she heard the hum of an engine. Swiveling, she saw a boat approaching the dock. It seemed she and Kyle were being rescued.

Was it really a rescue, though...if you were being taken from paradise?

POOLSIDE, under the sun. In California, that was a combination of circumstances you could expect at just about any time. Kyle adjusted his sunglasses and watched the group of kids kicking their way across the pool.

"Feet up," he called. "Keep your feet up, and kicking."

"Yeah...up and kicking," Hollan echoed unenthusiastically. He didn't seem in the spirit of the Guppies today. For about a year now, Kyle and Hollan had been coaching the Guppies, the under-ten swim team, down at the local community center. Usually the job was a lot of fun. Today, however, it seemed Hollan and Jackie had experienced another run-in, and that wasn't doing a whole lot for Hollan's mood. Wearing his swim trunks, Hollan sat hunched in a lounge chair, slapping cocoa butter on his arms.

"She's driving me crazy," he said.

"What's new," Kyle said.

"You'd think we could decide on a place to live. What does she have against my apartment?"

"Couldn't say," Kyle said.

"She's complaining that it's a bachelor pad, and she can't live in a bachelor pad. Can you believe it?"

Kyle thought about Hollan's apartment—oversize stereo speakers, water bed, wet bar. "I can believe it," he said.

"She wants us to live in her apartment. I can't live in a place like that. It's way too feminine. Have you ever seen her bathroom?"

"No," Kyle said sourly. "How would I ever have seen Jackie Shaw's bathroom?"

"You should see it, man. Little shells all over the walls...seashells. Little soaps you can't get a grip on. Little matching towels she never wants you to use. What the hell good are towels if you're not supposed to use them? And why does everything have to be so damn *little?*"

"Beats me," Kyle said.

"Anywhere we live, the baby's gonna take over, anyway," Hollan said mournfully, slathering on more cocoa butter.

"Feet up," Kyle called.

"The question is, where *are* we gonna live?"

"Don't ask me," Kyle said. "You've already got me working on the honeymoon."

"Yeah...so how's that coming?"

Kyle thought about being stranded on an island with Toni. He wouldn't mind still being stranded. He didn't think Toni would agree.

"We're working on it," he said. "Nothing definite, yet."

"You have it bad for Jackie's sister, don't you?"

Kyle thought it over. "Discussed marriage," he said. "Her and me."

Hollan took off his sunglasses. "No kidding?"

"She didn't go for the idea," Kyle said.

"You asked Toni Shaw to marry you?"

"Not in so many words," Kyle elaborated. "Told her I'd considered it, that's all."

"Hell, it's amazing you got that far."

"Why so surprised?" Kyle asked.

"Man, you're the ultimate bachelor."

Kyle didn't like the sound of that. Any second now, and he'd find out *he* was living in a bachelor pad. He stood and walked to the edge of the pool. The Guppies were doing fine without him. He walked back again.

"So what'd she say?" Hollan asked.

"Told me that every time we start to get serious, I make a joke out of it. Told me I want to have it both ways—I toss the idea of marriage out there, but I give myself the option of reeling it back in again. Told me I was hedging my bets.''

"Maybe you are," Hollan said.

"You're one to talk."

"Hey, at least I'm willing to admit I love Jackie. It's everything else I'm not too sure about."

Kyle sat down. He leaned forward, propping his elbows on his knees.

"So," Hollan said. "Do you love her?"

"Good question," Kyle said.

"Better figure it out. If you can't tell a woman at least that much—that you love her—you're really in trouble."

Two girls in bikinis walked by and smiled at Kyle and Hollan. Hollan smiled back. Then his smile faded.

"I've given up a whole lot for Jackie. So why do I have to give up my apartment, too?"

Kyle was too smart to go down that road again.

"Feet up," Hollan called desultorily. He put his sunglasses back on. "You gonna take the Parker job?" he asked Kyle.

"Still considering it." Kyle thought about the island, and how it had captured his attention. But was that because of the job prospects, or because he'd been there with Toni?

"Heck, man, the office isn't the same without you. Come back to the partnership, Kyle."

"You know things have to change. I'm looking for something more…small-scale."

"You think outfitting a whole island is small?"

"It has the danger of getting too grandiose," Kyle admitted. "That's why I haven't said yes yet."

"Problem is, you're too good to stay small," Hollan said. "Big's coming after you, no matter what you do. So here's my idea—you come back to the partnership. We expand. We take on more architects. That frees you up to do the projects you really want. That way, you have big, but you have small, too. Pretty good, huh?"

"Pretty interesting," Kyle said.

"Think about it, man."

It seemed Kyle had a whole lot to think about these days. And, perhaps most of all, Toni Shaw.

# CHAPTER TWELVE

JACKIE HAD TAKEN OVER the road. Her hands on the wheel of Hollan's very expensive sports sedan, she let the rest of the world know she was coming. She honked at the slightest excuse. Sometimes she honked with no excuse. And she talked a mile a minute, as if every other driver could hear exactly what she was saying.

"Watch out, little guy…no you don't! That's *my* lane… Hel*lo,* did we forget our turn signal today?"

Toni sat in the passenger seat, cringing as Jackie took one of San Francisco's hills at a nosedive.

"In case you're wondering, it's just *fine* with Hollan when I borrow his car," Jackie said a bit defensively. "Of course, this *is* the first time I've actually borrowed it. We've cleared up that little misunderstanding about me buying my own car. What's the point? Two vehicles would be such a hassle to maintain. We've decided that from now on this is *our* car."

Toni detected a current of tension underneath her sister's voice, but maybe it was best to dwell on the positive. "Well," she said, "glad to hear you guys are getting along."

"Believe it or not, we *do* love each other, Toni."

"I believe you."

Jackie cut in front of a truck. "That's my right of way, thank you very much!"

Toni tried to relax a little. However, being in transit with her sister was not exactly a relaxing experience.

"Hollan's so funny the way he talks about this car," Jackie said. "He says it cost him 120K. When we're out riding around, he always talks about taking it up to 200K. And when I left today, he said not to take it over 50K. Is that adorable, or what?"

Toni glanced at the speedometer, and couldn't help cringing again. "Jackie, didn't you say we were having lunch at a 'nearby' restaurant?"

"Sit back and enjoy yourself. It's not every day I can convince you to come up to San Francisco and spend time with me. Now, tell all. Have you found our honeymoon yet?"

Toni thought about the island where only a few days ago she'd been stranded with Kyle. The island she hadn't wanted to leave...

"We're still working on it," she said.

"Toni, the countdown is on. Hollan and I really need that honeymoon."

"You make it sound like we should just be able to flit into a store somewhere and order, 'One honeymoon to go, please.' You and Hollan couldn't make a decision. Do you think it's any easier for Kyle and me? Especially when it's not even our own honeymoon!''

''My, my, aren't we worked up,'' Jackie said as she pressed the accelerator and went through a yellow. ''Kyle Brennan is certainly having an effect on you. I heard all about how he asked you to marry him.''

''What?'' Toni's voice came out in an undignified squeak.

''Hollan says that according to Kyle, it was a sort of hypothetical marriage proposal, something just to let you know he'd been considering the idea. Frankly, I'd look into that, if I were you. A man either asks you to marry him, or he doesn't.''

Toni felt her cheeks burning. ''Kyle Brennan did *not* ask me to marry him. It was all…a joke. I asked him, very sarcastically, if he was proposing marriage, and then—''

''So you're the one who brought the subject up.''

Toni was tempted to yell. Instead, she managed to speak calmly. ''Kyle and I were only discussing marriage in a very…a very *hypothetical* way. No one proposed to anybody.''

''Are you in love with him, Toni?''

''Of course not,'' she answered too quickly. ''How could I be in love with Kyle Brennan?''

"Oh, I dunno," Jackie said. "Handsome, witty, intelligent, kind, successful, rich...want me to stop?"

"Please do," Toni said stiffly. "I'm not in love with the man. More to the point, he's not in love with me."

"Are you so sure about that?" Jackie honked as she sailed past a station wagon going slow in the fast lane.

"Kyle doesn't want to be in love," Toni said, surprising herself with the insight. "In his own way he's as much a cynic as I am. All he's had lately is bad luck with women. He doesn't want any more bad luck."

"What a pair the two of you are," Jackie said in a condescending voice. "Toni, there is nothing in this world like being in love, absolutely nothing. You think you were in love with Full-of-Himself Greg, but wait till you experience the real thing."

"Jackie, you can't even decide on your own honeymoon, so please don't lecture me—"

"Hollan and I," Jackie said relentlessly, "no matter what our difficulties, are fated to be with each other. We *know* what love is...real love. Now, tell me what time it is."

There were moments when Toni could cheerfully throttle her sister. This was one of those moments. Nonetheless, she looked at the crystal-gauge clock on the dash.

"It's eleven fifty-eight. I wish we'd just get to the damn restaurant—"

"Better take your phone out of your briefcase," Jackie said. "It's going to ring any minute."

"What are you talking about?"

"Just take it out, Toni. For once, don't be difficult."

"Difficult," Toni grumbled. "I'll tell you who's difficult." She unbuckled her briefcase and took out her phone. It chirped. Toni glanced at her sister.

"Go ahead, answer it," Jackie said.

Toni gave her sister another suspicious glance, then put the phone to her ear.

"Hello. Toni Shaw."

"Ms. Shaw, this is Laurence Allingdale."

Toni raised her eyebrows. "Laurence Allingdale of Allingdale, Reed and Mathews?"

"I see you've heard of us."

What lawyer in the San Francisco area *hadn't* heard of the very exclusive law firm of Allingdale, Reed and Mathews?

"Yes, Mr. Allingdale," Toni said, somehow managing to sound nonchalant. "What can I do for you?"

"Perhaps it is what I can do for you, Ms. Shaw. Your charming sister interviewed me for a newscast the other day, and she happened to mention that you are a very promising young lawyer. She also informed me that you have been quite unhappy as a public defender."

Toni opened her mouth to protest, but no words came out. The smooth voice of Laurence Allingdale continued.

"You might be just the type of talent we like to recruit. Speak to my assistant, Ms. Shaw—he'll make an appointment for you to come see us."

Toni was still trying to formulate a protest when the assistant came on the line. Before she knew it, she had an appointment for Friday afternoon.

Jackie looked smug as she cut in front of a van and gave two impudent honks of the horn. "Sometimes," she said, "I'm amazed at the advantages of being *me*. I meet all kinds of wonderful people—people like Mr. Laurence Allingdale. Isn't it wonderful, Toni? I may just have changed your entire life!"

THAT FRIDAY, Kyle sat across from Toni's mother in a San Francisco café. He'd run into Marianne Shaw a short while ago at Ghiradelli Square. Kyle had simply been wandering, trying to figure out what he was going to do next with his life. He'd been taking too many such walks of late. But then he'd bumped into Toni's mother coming out of a shop. Marianne had put on a cheerful facade, talking about the gift she'd just purchased for a friend, yet underneath she'd seemed worried and distracted. Kyle supposed that was why he'd ended up suggesting lunch: Toni's mother seemed so unhappy.

Now she continued to look worried.

"Mrs. Shaw," said Kyle at last, "is everything all right with your family—is everything all right with Toni?"

"She's fine. Except for dating that dismally dull Dan."

"Right," Kyle said. "Good old Dan Greene."

Marianne sipped her drink, a cherry fizz. "Mr. Brennan—Kyle—my oldest daughter is a very lovely, complex young woman. I'm afraid the rather jaded attitude she's developed is something of a defense. Someone broke her heart not too long ago—but you know about that, too, I'm sure?" She didn't wait for an answer; she seemed to be warming to the subject. "Underneath the sharp edges, Toni is very intense. Perhaps too intense. When she loves someone, she gives too much of herself, I think. And so she sees only two alternatives—give everything or give nothing."

Apparently Toni had put him in the "give nothing" category.

Marianne Shaw was perusing him astutely. "I can't help thinking you would be good for my daughter, Kyle. It's a pity she doesn't see things my way." Marianne paused. "Not that I'm an expert at personal relationships," she said in a low voice. "Even after all my years of marriage...I'm still no expert."

"Maybe nobody is," said Kyle. The waitress

brought their food—salad nicoise for Marianne, red snapper for Kyle. Marianne poked at her salad, then set down her fork and sighed.

"I'm afraid I'm not very good company today," she said. "You see, I do have something on my mind. My husband wants me to leave everything behind and go off with him around the world. Just when I have things the way I like them, he wants to go off. Tell me, Kyle, what is it about you men and jaunting?" She gazed at him almost accusingly.

"Well, I can't speak for the whole male species, Mrs. Shaw."

She sighed again. "If I could at least understand what Charles is thinking—why he feels the need to be a world explorer—that would be a start."

Kyle didn't know about Charles Shaw, but he ended up saying what had been on his own mind lately. "You begin to think you've missed out. You spend years and years building up a life, a career, and then you wonder if you went in the right direction. You start thinking about all the roads you didn't take."

Kyle didn't imagine he'd given the best insight in the world. But Marianne Shaw looked very intent as she thought over what he'd said.

"I love my husband a great deal," she said, her voice quiet. "I want him to be happy. I know, of course, that the bank hasn't given him everything he's needed. Oh, it's been a good career, and a good living for our family. But I'm very aware that it hasn't fulfilled something deeper in Charles. He's looking for something more—but I'm afraid he's not so sure what that something is, himself. He thinks perhaps he'll get it by going somewhere different—somewhere exotic. But what will happen if nothing works? What if he needs to find something inside himself—not something in Tasmania or Tangier?''

Kyle was no marriage counselor. But in a way, Marianne reminded him of his own mom. Both women had the same earnestness, the same concern for their husbands…maybe even the same puzzlement about what made their husbands tick.

''I'll tell you a story about my dad,'' Kyle said after a moment. ''He's an engineer, but all his life what he's really wanted to do is ranch. Every time he tries it, though, something goes wrong. Once he invested in a spread that went belly up. Another time he went to help my uncle with roundup, and broke his arm in a disagreement with a cow. It's like he's jinxed. My mother keeps trying to get him to quit. Tells him to be happy with what he is—an engineer who's real good at his job, even if he never finishes any projects around the house. But my dad won't listen. He still wants to be a rancher. No one—not even my mom— can talk him out of it.''

Marianne gave a slight smile. ''Are you telling me, Kyle, that when a man's determined to do something, his wife shouldn't waste her time trying to convince him otherwise?''

He contemplated his tequila sour. ''Maybe some people—male or female—are particularly bull-headed.''

''Maybe so,'' Marianne said. ''Maybe they have to travel those roads not taken, and if some of the roads turn out to be dead ends, well, they have to find that out for themselves, don't they?'' She still sounded unhappy. ''The thing is, Kyle, maybe I have a few of those roads to explore myself. When you hit your fifties, you realize you don't have all the time in the world left. And you realize you'd better start thinking over your options. Choices left behind, the things you could have done but never did.''

''Maybe it's not too late,'' Kyle said, more to himself than to Marianne. ''Maybe you can go back and take the road you missed the first time.''

If only he believed that.

SATURDAY AFTERNOON, Toni knocked on the door to Kyle's town house. Then she resisted the urge to turn around and walk away. She was here on business, she reminded herself. Honeymoon business.

Kyle opened the door, and without a word he took her hand and drew her inside. Then he kissed her.

It was a kiss that made her tingle all the way down to her toes. It took away her breath, made her weak in the knees. She barely managed to hang on to her briefcase.

When at last Kyle released her, she had the alarming desire to grab hold of him all over again.

"Darn it, Kyle, why'd you do that?"

He gave her a smile that sent another tingle through her. "Couldn't stop myself," he said.

She pushed a hand distractedly through her hair. "When we talked on the phone, you promised..."

He smiled again. "I don't remember making any promises not to kiss you."

"You promised," she said sternly, "to do things my way this time."

"And your way means...no kissing?"

"Exactly." She felt silly, but she repeated it. "No kissing."

"On my honor," he said, very solemn. "No more kissing."

She flushed, feeling sillier than ever. "Kyle," she said, "aren't you going to leave me any dignity at all?"

"Dignity is overrated," he said imperturbably as he ushered her into the living room.

It was a relaxed, comfortable sort of place. There was a big sofa in navy blue corduroy, two armchairs that didn't match, a faded Persian rug. Toni sat down on the sofa. But then she stood up again.

"Maybe this isn't such a good idea," she said.

"We have to come up with a honeymoon somehow," he said. "We figured the island wasn't right for Jackie and Hollan."

"Not right at all." Toni tried not to think about the island. Because every time she *did* think about it, all she wanted was to go back there with Kyle. "For crying out loud," she grumbled, "why are we still giving in this way? We should just tell them to find their own blasted honeymoon, and be done with it."

"I think it was something about you having a soft spot for your sister. And me having a soft spot for you."

Toni decided to ignore the last part of his remark. "Yesterday Jackie showed me an ultrasound picture of the baby, and I turned to mush. In less than six months I'll be a bona fide aunt."

"Hmm, ultrasound. Hollan did mention something about nearly fainting when they took a photo of the baby. I thought he had lost his mind."

"Lord, I'd hate to see him in the labor room," Toni said. "Except that's the latest controversy."

"Yeah, I heard," Kyle said. "Hollan swears that when the time comes, no way can he make it through the birth."

"And Jackie swears he'd better be there every second, or she'll never speak to him again." Toni shook her head. "We're actually trying to come up with a honeymoon for these people?"

"That's the idea."

Toni sat down again.

"Want something to eat?" Kyle asked. "Never discuss honeymoons on an empty stomach, that's what I always say."

Toni had promised herself this afternoon would be all business, but somehow she ended up saying yes to bologna sandwiches and a bag of microwave popcorn. Kyle dumped the popcorn into a big bowl and sat down next to her on the couch so they could share it. Very cozy...too cozy.

Toni moved to put a little distance between them. "You're an architect," she said, "but you live in a place that's really an apartment. Haven't you designed a house for yourself, Kyle?"

"No...only one for you."

That was something else Toni knew she shouldn't think about. "I'm serious," she said. "You ought to design a house for yourself. Maybe it's not just your career bothering you. Maybe you need a more permanent place to live."

He glanced around. "Thought this had the look of permanent."

"No...sorry. A town house is a compromise. Sure, it's more than an apartment, but it hasn't made a commitment to anything yet. Frankly, I don't see you as the town-house type."

He seemed interested. "What type am I?"

She wished she hadn't started this line of conversation. "I don't know. Maybe you're the country-manor type."

"Country manor...I like the sound of that."

Toni refused to look at him. She wiped her buttery fingers on a napkin and proceeded to unbuckle her briefcase. "We have to get to work," she said, pulling out a stack of brochures. "I stopped by a travel agency and collected these. They're for several resorts, hotels and vacation spots. We'll go through them, eliminate the ones that don't seem promising and then—"

"Toni," Kyle said, "how can you find a honeymoon by a process of elimination?"

"There was a little something said about doing this my way," she reminded him. "Your approach hasn't worked so far—the intuitive let's-just-see-how-we-feel approach."

"Actually, I thought it worked pretty well," he said.

She made the mistake of briefly closing her eyes. And there, shimmering in her mind, was the image of a gray-shingle mansion, ocean waves lapping against the shore...

Toni opened her eyes and handed Kyle some of the brochures. "Here," she said. "Look at the pictures, and see how they make you feel. That should make you happy."

Obligingly, he took the brochures and began to flip

through them. "No...not this one...nah..." An increasing number landed in the rejects pile.

"You're not taking this seriously," she said.

"Sure I am," Kyle said. "Look at this one, Toni. They posed a bunch of people around a swimming pool and told them to act like they were having a good time. No imagination." Another brochure tossed.

"This one's perfect," Toni said, opening a pamphlet and pointing to a photo of a couple aboard a sailboat. "Okay, maybe these people look a little too much like models, but that's beside the point. I think Jackie and Hollan would both enjoy sailing."

Kyle didn't even give the brochure a chance. He took it from Toni and lobbed it onto the rejects. "Here's the only place so far with any potential," he said, showing her a photo of a deserted beach down the coast. No one posing, no one pretending to have a good time, just lovely white sands and deep blue waves lapping against the shore.

She tossed *that* brochure onto the rejects. "Here's the problem," she told Kyle. "You keep choosing places that are too isolated. First Honeymoon Ranch, and then the island. But that type of atmosphere won't work for Jackie and Hollan. I'm sure they'd like to have more action, more people around them. And room service, of course."

"But *you* don't need room service," Kyle murmured. "You said you'd be happy to pitch your sleeping bag, and spend all day on the beach."

Toni found herself gazing into his eyes. She could feel her pulse beating, as if in response to the look he gave her.

She stood up so suddenly that she sent brochures scattering. Moving to a safe distance, she looked out one of the windows. On the opposite side of the street were some of San Francisco's famous "painted ladies"—quaint old houses spruced up in bright colors. Beyond were modern high-rises, but even those were bathed in shades of lavender and rose.

"That time we spent on the island, Kyle, I was only imagining what a honeymoon could be like. I'm smart enough not to wish for the real thing."

"Greg—the guy who broke your heart—I guess he offered you a honeymoon that didn't come through."

She brought her arms close against her body. "Oh, sure, we had the honeymoon all planned," she said in a brittle voice. "We were going to fly to Paris—we even had the tickets." She took a deep breath. "I know what you're going to say, Kyle. You're going to say that I'm not over him yet. But you're wrong about that. The only thing I'm not over is my incredibly bad judgment. How can I ever trust my own feelings when I chose someone who'd betray me?"

Kyle didn't answer. He just gave her one of his

thoughtful looks. She turned away from him and gazed out the window again.

"Anyway," she said briskly, "I have a lot of other things to think about. Such as my interview yesterday with Allingdale, Reed and Mathews."

Kyle didn't say anything for another minute, but then, to Toni's relief, he went with the change of subject.

"Tell me all about Allingdale, Reed and Mathews, big-time lawyers."

"I figured you'd probably heard of them," Toni said.

"Who hasn't? If there's a high-profile case anywhere, seems they're involved."

"Well, Jackie interviewed Laurence Allingdale for a story. And somehow it came out I was unhappy as a public defender, and might be looking for a change. Next thing I know, I'm sitting in the office of Laurence Allingdale himself. Possibility of a job offer, etcetera, etcetera."

Kyle settled back on the couch. "If it pans out, will you take it?"

She made a restless gesture. "It's tempting. And it's not just the money...or the prestige...although, believe me, it might be nice to know what a little prestige is like. But these people take cases that actually make a difference. And that's what I've been missing, Kyle.

The sense that somehow, in some small way, I *am* making a difference.''

"What about Sarah Martin?" Kyle, as usual, knew how to get right to the heart of the matter.

"Sarah...I went to see her yesterday, after I got back from my big appointment with Mr. Allingdale. And I tried hard to get through to her. I tried everything I knew so she'd tell me what really happened the night her baby died. But she wouldn't budge. Without actually admitting she was guilty, she wanted me to believe that she was. She's like someone turned to stone—someone who doesn't care about anything anymore. You asked if I've made a difference with Sarah...and no, it doesn't seem I have."

"Maybe a job with Allingdale is the road not taken," Kyle said. Toni gave him a puzzled glance. He stood and came over to her. "The road not taken— it's something I was talking about with your mother."

She frowned. "What on earth—"

"We had lunch yesterday, your mother and I."

Toni stared at him. "Kyle, please don't tell me that you and my mom are...buddies."

"Said she needed some advice."

"What kind of advice?"

"You'll have to ask her about that," he said maddeningly. "But you came up during the conversation."

"You talked about *me?*"

"Can't discuss that, either," he said, that unmistakable glint of humor in his eyes. "But we also talked about roads not taken. How we make choices, then wonder about the chances we let by."

Toni didn't understand how it happened, but now Kyle was holding her hand. His touch confused even as it tantalized.

"How wonderful that you and my mother had a chat. But we really do have to decide on a honeymoon, Kyle. I have to get back to Heritage City soon."

"Hmm, Saturday night," he said. "Guess you have a date with good old Dan."

She flushed. "I wish you wouldn't call him that. And anyway, Dan and I have been kicking around the idea of not dating anymore."

Kyle grinned. "You broke up with the guy."

"Well, I wouldn't exactly put it that way, but..."

"Antonia, I've just figured something out. You and I need to go on a date. For us, that's the road not taken."

"Would you stop with the roads—"

"It's the truth," he said. "We met, and we skipped right to the looking-for-a-honeymoon phase. We need to go back and start at the beginning. And that means we should go on a date. Save next Saturday for me." The humor was still in his eyes, his voice.

"Kyle, very funny, but I am *not* going on a date with you."

"Aren't you?" he murmured, and now somehow he was holding both of her hands. This time she didn't even try to pull away. She had the dismaying sensation that she was actually going to agree.

Against all her better judgment, it seemed she just might end up on a date with Kyle Brennan.

# CHAPTER THIRTEEN

PRIVACY WAS NOT a luxury afforded by the county jail. Toni stood by the large window offering a view into the visiting room, and gazed inside at Sarah Martin and her mother. Under other circumstances, she would have turned away, allowed mother and daughter at least the semblance of a private conversation. But right now she needed any clue at all that would help her with this case. If that meant behaving like a spy—so be it.

She couldn't hear what was being said. But she could see the way Denise Martin leaned toward her daughter, tried to put her arm around the girl. Sarah stiffened and pulled away. She kept her head bent, scarcely looking at her mother. Denise went on speaking, gesturing emphatically now and then, as if using every means she knew to reach her daughter. Apparently it was no use. Sarah sat in her chair, hands held motionless in her lap. She did not move or speak. She seemed to have removed herself to someplace no one could reach—not her mother, not Toni. Not anyone.

After a while, the guard came to escort Sarah back

to her cell. Toni waited a few moments, then went into the room and sat down at the table across from Denise Martin.

Denise, a woman in her mid-forties, possessed all the feminine ornaments her daughter lacked. Her hair was softly waved, her dress a pretty flower print, her nails manicured a shade of pale rose that perfectly complemented her lipstick. But the expression on her face was brittle, and her eyes welled with unshed tears.

Toni handed Denise a tissue and the woman carefully blotted her eyes.

"Mrs. Martin," Toni said, "you and I need to talk."

"I've already told you that I'll do anything I can to help my daughter."

"I want you to tell me about the day your grandson died," Toni said.

Denise clenched her hand on the tissue. "We've been over and over that. And every time, I tell you the same thing. My husband and I were gone all afternoon. We came home in the evening, only to find the police already there. Everything...everything had already happened."

Denise Martin was hiding something. Toni was sure of it. She could see it in the way the woman turned her head away each time she talked about that night. She could hear it in the way Denise's voice subtly changed. But, no matter how many times Toni queried her, the story was always the same.

Maybe it was time for a new tack. "Mrs. Martin," Toni said as gently as possible. "We both want what's best for your daughter. I need to understand Sarah, need to know every detail about her. Perhaps you can tell me more about her childhood. For example, how she reacted when her real father died—"

"My husband is her real father," Denise said rigidly. "He has been since she was eight years old. He adopted her. He gave her his name."

Toni rephrased. "Her biological father, then. Can you tell me about him?"

"He was an average man, and he died when Sarah was only three. You already know the facts."

"Facts...yes," Toni said. "But emotions...no." She didn't speak for a moment, letting Mrs. Martin think about what Toni was saying. "Even a child as young as three is affected by an event that traumatic," Toni went on. "And it must have been terrible for you, losing your first husband like that."

Denise Martin placed both hands on the table and stared down at them. She looked as if she was getting ready to repeat all the statements she'd uttered before, the sentence that always seemed too carefully rehearsed. But this time Denise surprised Toni. When she spoke, she faltered a bit, searching for words as if, for once, she had no script to guide her.

"When he got sick, I didn't believe it at first," she said in a low voice. "My Paul…how could he be that sick? I said he was an average man—but that's not fair to Paul. He loved me, I believe, even though he was way too young when we got married—and way too young to die. Only thirty. You're not supposed to get sick until you're old. That's what we believed anyway." She drew in her breath. "Oh, when he was gone—I thought I would die, too. Even with Sarah to care for, I didn't want to go on." She raised her face and stared at Toni. There was a bleakness in her eyes. "Ms. Shaw, have you ever lost someone like that?"

"No," Toni said. "Not like that."

"You know what I keep telling myself? If only Paul had lived, then everything would be so different. Sarah wouldn't be here, in this terrible place. And I wouldn't be here, talking to you. But Paul didn't live, did he? He died…he left me and Sarah. I was angry at him for the longest time because of that. I was so damn furious at him for leaving us…"

Denise Martin bent her head. She didn't speak for what seemed a very long time. But, at last, she lifted her head again.

"Almost five years Sarah and I were alone. It was hard. The money problems we had, that was one thing, but the loneliness was worse. And then…Rob came along. He rescued us. Sarah and I were living in that horrid little apartment, and I had that job I hated. And then one morning Rob walked into my life. So full of confidence, he was, and hope. I'd forgotten about hope. Rob gave it back to me. And he gave us a home—a real home.''

Toni thought about the Martin house, and how dreary it seemed. But, perhaps to Denise it had been a haven compared to where she'd been living.

''I can't lose hope…not again,'' Denise said in a voice so low Toni had to strain to catch the words. ''Somehow it has to come right again. I have to make it come right.'' Denise Martin sat in silence for another long moment. She seemed to have forgotten all about Toni's presence. Finally she stood and went toward the door. But then she glanced back at Toni.

''Ms. Shaw, maybe nobody knows the truth about the day my grandson died. But you know something? I don't care about the truth anymore. I just want…I just want hope.'' And with that, she walked out of the room.

IT WAS SATURDAY AGAIN…the Saturday Kyle had claimed. He'd asked Toni to go on a date with him— and she'd said yes.

She still couldn't believe she'd agreed to it. But here she was, rummaging wildly through her closet, frantically trying to decide what to wear. She was in a tizzy, as Jackie would say.

Toni finally sat on her bed, telling herself to calm

down. Why was she in such an uproar? First of all, Kyle had instructed her to dress "casual." Second, she'd already managed to convince herself she wasn't falling in love with the man. Third...it was only a date.

She began to feel better. She went through her closet again, and managed to decide on an outfit: the black jeans that always gave her an extra boost of confidence, a pin-striped shirt, her best belt with the hammered silver buckle. A silver bracelet and silver earrings for a touch of elegance and, for a touch of fun, her black-and-lavender sneakers.

It was only three o'clock in the afternoon, but Kyle had told her he wanted to start their date early. She heard a knock on her door just as she was applying a spritz of perfume and a dab of lip gloss. She went to the door, then hesitated. Last week, when she'd visited Kyle's town house, he'd greeted her rather more enthusiastically than she'd been prepared for. She wasn't ready for a repetition. At last, however, she opened the door cautiously and peered around it at Kyle.

"Hello," she said.

"Hello," he answered. "You don't have to be afraid to let me in. I'm not one of those guys who expects a kiss on the first date."

"Oh, for crying out loud," she said, swinging the door wide. He stepped over the threshold, his gaze lingering appreciatively on her.

"Just right," he said.

As far as compliments went, it was admirably restrained. So why did she feel flustered all of a sudden? *Calm down,* she reminded herself firmly. *It's only a date.*

She couldn't deny that Kyle looked "just right," too. He wore gray pants and a bottle-green polo shirt that made his hair look darker and richer than ever. Toni gave herself a limited time to gaze at him, and then she grabbed her jacket.

"I'm ready," she said.

"No briefcase?" he asked.

"Believe it or not, I don't normally carry my briefcase on a date. Wallet and keys in my front pocket, comb in my back."

"I like a woman who can travel light," Kyle said. A few moments later he'd escorted her downstairs and she was climbing into his convertible. Then, a few moments after that, they were headed north on the highway. Toni didn't even ask where they were going. She'd let him surprise her.

"So," Kyle said, "you really broke up with good old Dan."

"Not that it was necessary to break up formally," Toni muttered. "Dan and I never agreed to see each other exclusively. We never went to...the next level."

"The next level," Kyle repeated. "Kind of sounds like climbing stairs."

"A relationship should progress slowly," Toni said.

"Yeah, but not so slow you fall asleep along the way."

Toni tried not to remember the time she'd fallen asleep while at the movies with Dan. "Taking time is a good thing," she said. "And yes, a relationship *should* have levels."

"You and me, Antonia…what level are we on?"

She pushed a strand of hair out of her face. "No level, Kyle."

"Not even the first level?"

"Afraid not," she said firmly.

"You're so sure this date of ours is a one-time thing?"

"It seems to be some sort of experiment you're trying," she said. "I'm game for one day, but after that…no more dates."

"Sounds kind of like the no-kissing rule," Kyle observed.

Toni settled back against the headrest, enjoying the cool fall breeze. "Make fun all you like, Kyle. But this is it—one date."

"Well," he said, "guess we'd better make it a good one."

When they reached San Francisco, Kyle stopped near Golden Gate Park. He opened the trunk and brought out two kites. Unexpected, yes…and just right.

Toni couldn't remember the last time she'd been kite-flying in Golden Gate Park. She knew only that today it was a perfect activity. There was just enough of a breeze to send the kites sailing. Toni spooled out her string and felt just a bit as if she were soaring, too. Hadn't she felt this way before with Kyle? The day they'd flown to the island, of course.

She forgot to pay attention, and her kite came tumbling to the grass. She plunked herself down beside it and watched Kyle. He seemed to be having a grand time. There was another kite-flyer who wandered over beside him, a little boy who was getting his string in a snarl. Kyle stopped to help, and soon the boy's kite was back in the air. Toni felt the oddest constriction inside. What would it be like to watch your husband and child in the park? To know they both belonged to you…to have your own small family…

Kyle came over to her. "Feeling all right?" he asked. "You look as if you've been seeing ghosts."

She almost laughed at that. "Ghosts of the future, maybe? Somehow I don't think so. But don't ask me to explain, Kyle."

He didn't press the matter. Instead he grabbed her hand and pulled her up to stand beside him. "A walk through the park is next in order."

"This park? It's endless. We could be wandering around for days."

"Maybe that's the idea," he said.

And so they wandered. Skaters swerved past them, children dodged back and forth on the paths. But Kyle and Toni took their time. They paused to watch an elderly man and a young boy who were playing a game of checkers on one of the benches. They sat on their own bench and watched passersby. They got up and walked again, only to have their attention captured by a group of kids playing tag football. There were boys and girls both, and they appeared to be having a grand time. Why was it that everywhere Toni turned today, she seemed to see children? And, whenever she saw them, she felt an ache of longing inside.

"Want to talk about it?" Kyle asked as he studied her face.

"It's nothing," she said too quickly.

"Then why do you look so sad?"

"I'm not sad," she told him. "It's just that...I think I'm a little too affected by Jackie having a baby. It makes me hypersensitive to the issue of kids. I start to think about having one myself. Ridiculous, really, when you think about where I am in life. Not sure where I'm going with my career, living in an apartment, all of it."

"At least you don't need a husband," Kyle said. "That's what you told me, anyway. Nix on the husband, yea on the kids."

"I didn't mean I planned to go out and have kids *without* a husband," Toni said grumpily.

"So you figure maybe you need a husband, after all. Sort of as a necessary inconvenience—if you want kids, that is."

Toni gave him an aggravated look. "Do you feel obligated to poke holes in everything I say, Kyle?"

"Pretty much." He took her hand and drew her onward again. "Seems you've got a real puzzle," he said. "You want kids, but it'd be a hassle without a husband—then again, a husband would be a hassle, too."

"I'm sure I'll figure something out," Toni said dryly. Then, however, she saw a solemn little girl out-fitted in skates and knee pads, and she felt those yearn-ings again. "Damn," she said under her breath. "Kyle, let's just go do something else. The museum, that sounds good."

The park's art museum was located only a short distance away, and provided a welcome distraction. Toni tried to lose herself in one painting after another. It was starting to work—she was starting to get some control—when she saw a young couple, arms wrapped around each other, gazing dreamily at each other in-stead of appreciating the art. And that was all it took for Toni to feel a different kind of longing.

"This is absurd," she muttered to herself. And then, to Kyle, "What do you say we get something to eat? I'm hungry."

They left the park and ended up at a restaurant facing the bay. They were seated next to the windows, and beyond they could see boats clustered at their moorings, early evening casting a blue-gold light on the water. A bouquet of pink amaryllis made a centerpiece on the teakwood table. Kyle had chosen this place, and like everything else about the day it was just right. So why did Toni continue to feel these restless yearnings?

Perhaps she already knew the answer. Being around Kyle made her think about all the things she didn't see possible right now. Love…a family of her own…

"Maybe going on a date wasn't such a good idea," she said. "Maybe we could decide that it isn't really a date, after all."

"Can't do that, Antonia. Once you start a date, it's a date to the very end." He reached across the table and clasped her hand. She'd been doing this a lot today—holding hands with Kyle Brennan. That was the problem with a date. It made you feel as if holding hands was inevitable.

Dinner was a feast of grilled shrimp, deep-fried prawns and scallops, new potatoes, artichokes and capers, chocolate tart with hazelnut. Afterward, Toni and Kyle wandered along the shorefront, listening to the creak of the boat masts and the gentle slap of waves against the hulls. By now night had fallen, enveloping them in velvet darkness, even as lights shimmered upon the water. Somehow they were holding hands again.

*I don't want this day to end.* The thought came unbidden into Toni's mind. She could not deny it, though. She wanted to linger with Kyle, wanted to be with him. It seemed he felt the same way, too, because next they went to a dance club where a band played songs from the 1950s. Fast numbers, but lots of slow ones, too, where Toni found herself lost in Kyle's arms.

She didn't know how much time had passed. She knew only the feel of him next to her as they moved to the music. They didn't speak. There didn't seem any need for words.

The evening could not go on forever, of course. Midnight came, and finally they were headed back to Heritage City. Kyle had put up the top of the convertible. The car was snug and warm as the miles flew under the wheels. All too quickly they reached Toni's apartment.

*No...I don't want this to end.* Toni found herself fighting for more time.

"Would you like to come up for coffee?" she asked somewhat awkwardly. "Brewed this time. Not instant."

"If it's brewed, I'm definitely game."

For once, she was grateful that he kept a light tone. She felt a new tension between them as she led the way up the stairs and into her apartment. She tried to ignore it as she put the coffee on and busied herself with mugs and napkins. Kyle settled on a stool across the counter.

"So, was going on a date so bad?" he asked.

"It was actually very…nice."

"The thing about a first date," he said, "is that it makes you start thinking about a second date. Toni, I'd really like to see you again."

She clattered a spoon into a mug. "Haven't we taken this far enough? We're going to see each other plenty. We still have to find a honeymoon for Jackie and Hollan—"

"That's not a date, Toni. That's you and me trying to do a favor—however wacky—for your sister and my best friend."

Toni gazed into Kyle's dark brown eyes. "I thought tonight was just an experiment of sorts. Something to see what a date *would* be like between us. Well, now we've seen it."

"Didn't we discover anything?" he asked seriously.

"No—"

"We discovered we should go on a second date."

Toni wished the coffee wouldn't take so long. But finally it was ready, and she set a mug in front of Kyle.

"Okay," she said. "Here's how it is. Kyle, I don't want to fall in love with you. And if we keep…dating, there's a possibility that could happen. I'm sure, when it comes right down to it, you don't want the complication of...me falling in love with you.''

"I don't know," Kyle said with a grave expression. "Seems we'd finally be getting things in the right order. We date, we fall in love, we get engaged—*then* we look for a honeymoon.''

"There's one thing I can always count on with you,'' she said, stirring cream into her coffee. "No matter what subject we're discussing—marriage, honeymoons, *dating*—you'll make a joke out of it. Which is exactly why I don't want to fall in love with you, Kyle.''

"Maybe," he said. "Or maybe it's the fact that you're still in love with someone else.''

"I wish you wouldn't keep saying that. It's not true. I'm totally over Greg.''

Kyle gave her a reflective look. "Here's how I see it, Toni. One, you *do* have feelings for the guy. Two, you figure it's safer to believe all men are jerks than to trust your own judgment again. Three—''

"Two's enough," she said tightly.

"Three," he went on imperturbably, "you've got it all wrong if you think I'd ever do something like that...betray a woman after I'd asked her to marry me.''

Toni took a deep breath. "Kyle, for your information I don't think you'd do that at all. Frankly, I don't think you're the betraying kind. But I *do* think you hold back your emotions. Maybe you just don't want any more bad luck with women. Or maybe you're a little like me, after all. Maybe you believe love isn't the kind of thing that can last no matter how much you wish it could.''

Apparently he didn't have anything to say to that. He sat there drinking his coffee and looking discontented. After a few moments, Toni walked him to her front door. And suddenly she felt awkward all over again.

"Kyle, for what it's worth, I did enjoy our date. I enjoyed it very much. But it's over now, isn't it?''

"Not quite," he murmured, drawing her near. She placed her hands against his chest.

"Wait...I though you said no kisses on the first date...''

"I don't always keep my word," he said, and then he kissed her.

They kissed for a long moment. Toni put her arms around Kyle, allowing her fingers to tangle in his hair. And the thought came back, insistent and overwhelming. *I don't want this to end.*

What would be the harm in lingering? What would be the harm in holding him, and touching him, and letting this moment go on?

They lingered. They stood beside Toni's front door and turned the good-night kiss into something much more. Kyle gathered Toni so close she could feel the beat of his heart. She moved her hands over Kyle's shoulders, tangled her fingers in his hair once more. But, no matter how tightly they held each other, she could not seem to get enough of him.

Somehow she ended up leaning against the wall, arching her neck as Kyle kissed the pulse of her throat. A tantalizing, perilous warmth gathered deep inside her.

"Kyle," she murmured with an ache of longing.

"Do you want me to stop?" he asked, his own voice husky.

"No...not yet."

Could she steal another moment or two? Would it be so wrong? Later...later they would stop...

The settee was only a short distance from where they stood. Toni was the one who guided them there. She sank down with Kyle. They kissed again...and again. Kyle leaned Toni back against the cushions. The warmth inside her spread through every part of her.

"Kyle," she murmured, moving her hands over his back.

"You want me to stop...now?" His voice was huskier than ever.

"No...not yet." If only she could feel him a little closer to her—then she could stop...

She tugged his polo shirt from the waistband of his pants. And now she could feel his skin against her fingers. Now she could run her hands through that swirl of russet hair on his chest. She felt the intake of his breath, just before he kissed her once again.

His fingers moved over the buttons of her shirt. She helped him undo each button. He looked deep into her eyes. And this time he didn't have to ask the question out loud.

"No," she whispered. "Don't stop." The moment for that had passed. She had allowed this recklessness to take her, and carry her away. The warmth inside her had turned to heat, and she could not deny it.

A moment later, he drew her shirt away from her. Then he gently pulled down the straps of her bra, kissed the swell of her breasts. She gasped at the touch of his lips.

"Kyle...oh, Kyle..." She reached impatiently behind her back, unsnapped her bra, allowed the lacy material to fall away from her. And now he caressed her intimately, his eyes darkening all the more as he gazed at her.

"Toni," he murmured. "You're the most beautiful woman I've ever seen."

"I can't believe that..."

"Believe me." He kissed her throat once more, trailed kisses downward.

"Kyle...oh, Kyle..." She was repeating herself, she knew. But she loved repeating his name. It came from her lips upon a sigh of desire. And now he was the one who spoke her name, his own voice taut with desire.

"Toni...Toni..." He shifted, trying to bring her closer. "We're not maneuvering too well on this thing."

She laughed shakily. "I think settees were invented to keep couples from going too far."

"Toni, I want to go too far."

"I want it, too, Kyle," she whispered back. Too late...too late to stop...

She stood, held out her hand to him. Bare to the waist, she couldn't understand why she felt no shame, no embarrassment. But she wanted Kyle to look at her, wanted his gaze to caress her. He rose beside her, and together they moved to the bedroom. She turned on the bedside lamp, then sank onto the mattress. Kyle stretched out beside her. Their limbs entwined. It was luxury to hold each other now without impediment.

Kyle's hands moved over her skin. Everywhere he touched, she felt the heat of her own longings. Her fingers trembling, she unbuckled her belt, unzipped her jeans. Kyle helped her to pull them away from her body.

"Beautiful," he repeated, even as he slipped her underwear down her legs. And now, too, his pants came off...his briefs. Light from the lamp spilled over him, allowing her to see every masculine contour.

"Come close," she whispered. "Please..."

He held her and caressed her and kissed her. "Toni," he murmured at last. "You have something, don't you?"

"Something…" It took her a moment to surface from the swirl of her own desire. "Oh, Kyle. No…no birth control."

"Nothing?"

"I haven't needed it recently," she muttered. "Did you bring anything?"

"No," he said wryly, kissing her shoulder. "I didn't plan on this, Toni, believe it or not."

"You mean—between the two of us, we don't have a single thing?"

"Toni…there's lots of other things we can do. Trust me…let me show you."

He proceeded to show her, with his hands, his mouth, touching her and kissing her in the most intimate way. Toni had never known anything like this. So decadent. So delicious in every sensation evoked. She felt herself spinning out of control…until, at Kyle's command, she came with one ragged gasp after another.

"Oh…Kyle…" It seemed she had to keep saying his name.

He held her afterward, but he'd taught her something she had to try in return. She touched him, and then she trailed her own kisses down his body. She caressed him intimately with her mouth…

The pleasure she gave him seemed equal to her own. She heard it in the cries he could not keep back. And now, at last, both of them sated, they lay in each other's arms.

Only gradually did reality return to Toni. And only gradually did the truth occur to her.

To all intents and purposes, she and Kyle had just had sex on their first date.

## CHAPTER FOURTEEN

KYLE SAT IN A BOAT with Toni's father. The boat sat in the middle of a lake. Toni's father held a fishing pole, and he looked glum. Kyle held his own fishing pole, and felt glum. The fish weren't biting.

Kyle couldn't believe how he kept getting involved with Toni's family. He'd been assigned to locate a honeymoon spot for Toni's sister. He'd been to lunch with Toni's mother. And Toni's father had now invited him on this little excursion. What could happen next?

"You know," said Charles Shaw, "they stock this lake with trout, just to make sure weekend fishermen like us get a catch."

"Doesn't seem to be working," Kyle said.

"Think about it, though. Do you really want to fish in a lake where the trout are practically served up to you on a platter?"

Kyle observed his motionless fishing line. "No one's serving right now," he said.

"You get my point, though, Kyle. It's like skeet shooting in an aviary."

Kyle gave in. "Yeah, it's no fun when everything's prearranged for a 'natural' experience."

Charles nodded. "That's it, exactly."

"Especially when they stock the lake with fish smarter than we are," Kyle added.

Charles grinned. "You know something, Kyle? Seems to me like I've spent my entire life in situations just like this one. Sitting on a damn stocked lake. Where's the adventure in that?"

"Can't rightly see it," Kyle admitted.

"So you're wondering why I brought you here, if I don't like the damn lake."

Kyle had been wondering about the whole thing. It was Sunday, and this morning Toni's father had called him on the spur of the moment to go fishing. They'd ended up at this lake not far from Heritage City. It was a peaceful place, surrounded by willows and pines. But maybe it was too peaceful, as far as Charles Shaw was concerned.

"Trouble is," Charles said, "when you're only a weekend fisherman, you don't have time to go where you'd really like. You have to make do with whatever's close to home. Sticking close to home—that limits you."

Kyle wasn't so sure he agreed with that. He'd been sticking fairly close to home ever since he'd met Toni Shaw. They could never travel very far, because they had to find a honeymoon location close by. But they managed to use their imaginations wherever they went.

Take yesterday, for example, when they'd gone on their first "date." They'd had a good time doing the seemingly ordinary. Flying kites in the park...eating dinner by the bay...making love in Toni's apartment...

Afterward, she'd seemed determined to salvage any dignity she could. She'd insisted that they hadn't technically made love because they hadn't "gone all the way." And then, with this pronouncement, she'd booted Kyle out of her apartment.

Kyle never had been one to quibble about technicalities. As far as he was concerned, they'd made love, all right.

"The thing is," said Charles, "my dad stayed close to home all his life and I still can't figure out where it got him. When it comes down to it, he left only one thing behind—that piece of land in the wine country."

"Toni seems to think a lot of it," Kyle said.

"That she does," Charles agreed. He gave Kyle an astute look. "Too bad she won't let you design the house for her up there."

Maybe Charles Shaw had invited him here today to discuss Toni—find out if Kyle's intentions were honorable, and all that.

"Dan Greene is one of my best employees at the bank," said Charles. "Worked his way up onto the board in no time. But still, the guy's pretty dull. No...I'll never ask Dan to go fishing. Never thought my daughter would end up with someone like him. Always thought Toni was the one most like me—that she wanted a little adventure in her life.''

Kyle shifted the angle of his pole. He still hadn't lured any fish.

"Anyway," said Charles, "I didn't ask you here to talk about my daughter."

That was one question answered, at least.

"Thought maybe you could tell me what's gotten into my wife," Charles said gruffly. "She said she talked to you, and you made her realize she has to change her life. Yesterday she announced she's going back to school, and who the heck knows what else. Something about how she has to go down new roads, the roads never taken. Said you were the one who gave her the idea."

Kyle wished they could go back to discussing fish. "Mr. Shaw, the part about roads. It was a figure of speech—"

"Relax, I'm not blaming you. I'm just trying to figure out why my wife isn't jumping at the chance to do some real traveling for once. Why does she want to go sit in a classroom at this stage in her life? She's already had a satisfying career—she's counseled all those kids, made a difference in their lives. Okay, so she says she's always dreamed about getting her doctorate in psychology. I understand that. But when you could go to Nova Scotia or Brazil…why the heck would you pick a doctorate in psychology?''

Kyle rubbed his neck. He reminded himself, not for the first time, that he was no marriage counselor. Charles Shaw, however, was gazing at him from underneath his fishing cap with a beleaguered expression.

''Maybe Mrs. Shaw needs to see just how far she can go in her career,'' Kyle said. ''You've had your shot—made a mark for yourself in banking. Maybe if she doesn't take a chance, she'll always wonder what she missed.'' It was about as neutral a statement as he could make, but Charles appeared to give it a great deal of thought.

''Hell, I want Marianne to be happy,'' he said. ''She's got all these class catalogs, and she pores over them the way I look at my maps…if it's what she needs, I want her to have it. But I'm just about finished with my own career, Kyle. If I don't do something else, I'll bust. You ever felt that way?''

Kyle remembered how he'd felt at the thought of designing one more office building. ''Yes,'' he said, ''I know what you mean.''

They sat in silence for a few moments, lines dangling in the water. Then Charles went on.

''Here I am,'' he said, ''fifty-four years old. But you know something? I remember clear as yesterday how it felt to be twelve—or twenty. Back then I only wanted to be one thing—an explorer. Sounds kind of silly, doesn't it? But traveling around the world, seeing things I'd never seen before is what I wanted to do. A kid grows up, of course, becomes a young man. He goes to college and takes a degree in business. Tells himself it's a good degree, something maybe he can parlay into an overseas job. Then he gets his first big break, a job in a bank. Tells himself it's a step on the road to international banking. He'll get to see the world...and then he meets a young woman...the woman of his dreams...and traveling doesn't seem so important anymore.''

They sat in silence again. And Charles spoke again.

"I don't regret for a second all the years Marianne and I have spent building a life together. A home, a family. They've been great years, Kyle. But now, if I don't do some of the things I've always dreamed about, I'm afraid I'll end up like my father—dead and unsatisfied, never having gone much of anywhere. Trouble is, if Marianne doesn't come with me, it won't be the adventure I've always dreamed. When you love someone, that's the way you feel. Kind of puts a person in a bind. Know what I mean?''

Kyle imagined what it would be like to fall for a woman like Toni Shaw, and then to face a life without her.

"Yeah," he said, "I know what you mean.''

They sat. A breeze rippled over the lake. And then Kyle's line began to ripple.

"Hey, looks like you got one," Charles said. Kyle reeled in the line, and a small trout flip-flopped in the air. Both men contemplated it.

"Seems like a shame," Kyle said. "You're a fish, and someone dumps you in a lake just so someone else can hook you."

"Does seem like a shame," Charles agreed.

"You want the honors," Kyle said, "or should I?"

Charles reached over, unhooked the trout and sent it back into the water. And then, the rest of the afternoon, they sat without a word...and without a nibble.

TONI WROTE another few sentences on the blackboard in her office, then stepped back to study them. She was still trying to fit together the facts in the Martin case. The problem was, no one agreed on what the facts were. Even the specialists called in to consult on the case had conflicting opinions. One doctor stated that the child Jeremy Edward Martin had most likely died immediately after being severely shaken. Another doctor stated that the shaking could have occurred up to twelve hours before the little boy's death. Certainly this disparity complicated the matter of an alibi for Sarah Martin. Not that Sarah was helping Toni to construct an alibi. She stubbornly refused to participate in her own defense.

"Hello, Toni," said Kyle from the doorway.

She'd been expecting him—they'd arranged this get-together over the phone—but nonetheless her heart begin to pound absurdly.

"Hello, Kyle," she said, her voice formal. She didn't want to invite any discussion about what they'd done in her apartment three nights ago. Every time she thought about it, she felt her skin burn. How could she have let herself get so carried away?

She went to her desk and stacked some papers together. "I'm almost ready to go," she said. "Just finishing up some details."

He nodded toward the blackboard. "Any luck with Sarah Martin?" he asked. Obviously he didn't choose to discuss Saturday night, either.

She glanced at the blackboard in frustration. "No," she said. "No luck to speak of. Things just keep getting more and more confused. I still haven't been able to locate Sarah's boyfriend Richard. And Sarah's mother won't level with me. I can sense *she's* hiding something...not to mention that Sarah's completely given up on herself. I feel like my hands are tied. If your own client won't cooperate with you, how can you prepare even an adequate defense?" She went to the board, picked up the eraser and passed it over what she'd written. "There—blank," she said. "That's how the case is going."

"Any word from Messrs. Allingdale, Reed and Mathews?" Kyle asked.

"As a matter of fact...yes. This time it's been requested that I come in so Reed and Mathews can take a look at me, too. Apparently, no hiring decisions are made without all the partners involved."

"No actual offer yet?"

"Not yet," she said, "but if they actually *do* make one..." Her voice trailed off as she looked around her cramped office. Too many case files were piled willy-nilly on her desk—too many cases she didn't believe in. "I wonder, could I give all this up?" she said caustically. "Sarah Martin's mother said something the other day. She said that all she wanted was hope. I'm not sure what she meant for herself, but I know that's what I want—hope for my own work. I have a suspicion I'm not going to get it here."

"If you take a job with Allingdale et al., you'd probably have to move to San Francisco," Kyle said.

"No question about it. I couldn't possibly commute—not with the kind of caseload they'd be handing me. No such thing as an underworked lawyer, anywhere."

Kyle was obviously following a different train of thought. "Hmm...you in San Francisco, me in San Francisco...interesting..."

Toni had the uneasy conviction that he was going to bring up Saturday night, after all.

"Kyle, why don't you tell me about *your* career crisis," she said hastily. "What's new in the architectural biz?"

He gave her an amused glance, but obliged her. "Hollan keeps trying to talk me into coming back to the partnership. Under different circumstances than before—supposedly we'd hire some other architects to help take up the slack while I'm pursuing cream-of-the-crop designs. Sounds just a little too good to be true."

"Maybe it's not. Maybe it would be the perfect arrangement. Except, what about the island job?" As soon as she mentioned that, she wished she hadn't. The island always evoked impossible longings in her.

"I've had a few more talks with Russ Parker. Nothing solid yet, but we're kicking some ideas around. How I'd fit that in with everything else—who knows. But you don't really want to talk about architecture, do you, Toni? We both know Saturday night won't go away—"

"*Please* don't, Kyle. It'll go away if we don't mention it." Toni felt her skin heat up all over again. "So, let's get down to business." She reached into her briefcase, pulled out a brochure and handed it to him. "This is where we're going today. It's a resort not far from here, near Carmel. I made an advance phone call, checked everything out and I'd say it has great promise as a honeymoon spot. We're running out of time, you know. The wedding is in less than a month. We have to make a decision.''

He gave her a long look that did nothing to calm her heartbeat, or to soothe the flush on her cheeks. But at last he tucked the brochure into the pocket of his jacket.

''We'll do it your way, Antonia,'' he said. ''No talk about Saturday...for now.''

EARLY THAT EVENING, Toni whacked the birdie across the badminton net to Kyle. He returned it expertly.

''Is there anything,'' she said, ''that you don't know how to do?''

''Is there anything,'' he countered, ''that we haven't tried at this so-called resort? You've had us do everything. Tennis...billiards...backgammon...the worst part was the getting-to-know-you game of balloon volleyball in the lobby.''

''I thought that was a very nice touch by the management,'' said Toni. ''What better way to be introduced to the other guests?''

''I have a great idea,'' Kyle said. ''No introductions, period.''

Toni eyed him skeptically. ''I did notice the way you shredded your name tag. Not very sociable, if you ask me.'' Granted, she'd kept the two of them busy all afternoon. But it seemed best to stay occupied. That way they didn't have a great deal of time for conversation.

Now she set down the badminton racket and headed across the lawn to the croquet set.

"This time I know I can beat you at something," she said, picking up a mallet. With a satisfying *clunk* she knocked a ball through a wicket.

"I draw the line at croquet," he said.

"Just one game, Kyle."

"Just one," he conceded.

The game was close—very close. Kyle was competitive when it came to sports. So was Toni. Neither one of them gave an inch. They kept knocking each other out of bounds, but Toni was the one who reached the end post.

"Yes! I finally beat you at something, Kyle. It's a very satisfying feeling, let me tell you." She set down her mallet and glanced at her watch. "Good—we won't be late for the mixer in ballroom D." She began to head off across the lawn again, but Kyle took hold of her hand.

"Forget it," he said. "No mixer in ballroom D. No line-dance practice in ballroom C. No gin rummy in ballroom B. I need a break." He led her down a path toward the beach.

"Oh no," she said. "No beaches."

"Why not, Antonia?"

"Because the combination of you and a beach...I just don't think so, Kyle."

He didn't listen to her, and before she knew it, they were walking along the shoreline. Waves curled over the sand, and here and there strings of kelp had washed in from the ocean. A man strolled ahead of them, a black Scottie dog bouncing at his heels.

Kyle bent to take off his shoes and socks. Toni did the same. You couldn't possibly walk in the sand unless you had bare feet. It was an unwritten California law.

Dangling their shoes by the laces, they walked side by side. "Well," said Toni. "This resort has everything, doesn't it? Any activity you can think of, lots of friendly people and a very nice beach. I think we've found a honeymoon."

He took her hand once more. "I thought we found a honeymoon on the island."

"For us, maybe. Not for Jackie and Hollan—" She stopped, appalled as the sense of her own words became clear. "Kyle," she said, "I didn't mean we'd found a honeymoon for *us*. You can't possibly think I meant that."

He gave her his smile, the one that made her want to run her bare toes over his. "What's that old saying about Freudian slips, Antonia?"

"That doesn't apply here," she objected. "People

are allowed to make slips of the tongue without obscure meanings being read into them.''

''There wasn't anything obscure about it, if you ask me,'' he remarked solemnly. ''You said we'd found our honeymoon. That's fairly clear—''

''Kyle,'' she groaned.

''Okay, if we can't talk about our honeymoon, then at least we have to talk about Saturday night.''

She turned around and went back the direction they'd come. The waves lapped against her feet. ''Forget it, Kyle.''

''It happened, Toni. We made love.''

''No,'' she said stubbornly. ''We didn't. Not all the way. And what we *did* do was just so…so remarkably self-indulgent…''

''Don't you think there can be a whole lot of variety to sex?''

''There hasn't been a lot of variety for me in the past,'' she said, wondering why she felt the need to confess.

''Saturday was just a beginning for us.''

''No,'' she said. ''It doesn't have to be. It's still not too late—''

''Yes, it is, Toni. For me, anyway.'' All humor had vanished from his tone. He stopped, obliging her to stop also. She was trembling deep inside as he touched her chin with his finger, tilted her face so she had to look at him. ''Toni,'' he said. ''We took a step Saturday night, and I'm glad we did. Aren't you the one who told me that relationships advance in levels? I'd say we went to the next level that night. Now I want to go to the next.''

''And what level is that?'' she asked, half dreading, half desiring the answer.

''I want us to see each other,'' he said. ''On a regular basis. Not just one date. Not just two. And I want to make love to you a whole lot more. Maybe we'll find out if we're headed to the next level after that.''

''I don't like the sound of it,'' Toni said automatically. ''There aren't any guarantees about where we'll end up.''

''Nobody has guarantees, Toni. But I've been thinking about this a lot. Your father said something to me the other day, something about—''

''Oh no,'' Toni interrupted. ''Now you're having lunch with my father?''

''Not lunch. We went fishing.''

''Fishing,'' she echoed in disbelief.

''We caught one fish, but we put him back.''

Toni began walking again. ''I have this feeling my family wants to adopt you. Which is all well and fine, but that doesn't mean you and *I* should get together, Kyle.''

He kept pace beside her. ''Your dad said something about finding the woman of his dreams—your mother—and how after that no adventure can really be an adventure unless she's along.''

Toni tried to picture her normally uneffusive father confiding as much. ''I'm very glad to hear he feels that way. But what is this effect you have on my parents, Kyle?''

''Beats me. The point is, Toni, we'd better find out if we were meant to have adventures together.''

''We've already had some adventures. What you're really saying is…I'm supposed to figure out if you're the man of my dreams.''

''Something like that,'' he said.

This time she was the one who stopped walking. ''Don't you see, Kyle?'' she asked. ''Even if I *did* think you were the man of my dreams—even if we fell in love with each other right now, on this very spot—I wouldn't trust it to last.''

''You're afraid I'd hurt you,'' he said. ''Toni, I'll never make promises I can't keep.''

He made it all sound so logical. Safe, almost. Take one step at a time, see where it led. She was tempted.

She bent to put on her shoes and socks. Then she began taking the path back up to the resort buildings. ''I can't even think right now, Kyle. You want an answer, but I don't know what to say. I mean, what are you asking—you want to be my boyfriend?''

''That's what some people call it.''

''Oh, Lord,'' she muttered. What she needed at this

moment was some decisive action. If nothing else, she needed to finish up with this resort and head back to Heritage City. Maybe once she was at home, she *would* be able to think straight. Especially if Kyle wasn't around, distracting her.

She led the way to the main lobby and marched up to the registration desk. "Excuse me," she said to the receptionist. "Mr. Brennan and I would like to inspect one of your honeymoon suites now. If you remember, we're the people deciding on a honeymoon for Jackie Shaw—"

"Oh, certainly," said the woman. "Please tell Jackie I'm a big fan of hers. Here's a key to room 209. It has a wonderful balcony view. You're registered through tomorrow noon."

"There must be some misunderstanding," Toni said. "We didn't want to register for the night. We didn't want to register at all—"

"Compliments of the management," said the woman. "We want to make absolutely certain you enjoy your visit here, and see everything we have to offer." She lowered her voice conspiratorially. "Believe me, it would be quite a coup to have Jackie Shaw spend her honeymoon with us."

"No doubt," Toni said dryly. She didn't see the point of arguing. She and Kyle would just give the room a quick once-over, return the blasted key and be out of here.

A few moments later they'd located room 209, and Toni turned the key in the lock. "Can you believe it?" she asked. "They're actually trying to bribe us by having us spend the night."

"Mighty low-down," Kyle said. "This honeymoon committee can't be bought so easily."

Sometimes it really was best just to ignore Kyle. Toni went into the room and glanced around.

"Can't complain about the accommodations," she said. "From here, everything looks pretty good. Spiffy decor. Clean—don't see even a speck of dust. This place has my vote for sure."

"You're not being very thorough," Kyle said. "She mentioned something about the view—we have to check out the balcony."

Toni joined him on the balcony. "Okay, fine," she said.

"Toni...are you really giving it a look?"

She gazed out toward the limitless expanse of ocean and noted how the evening light worked its magic in hues of dusky peach and mauve. "Very nice," she said. "Now let's go."

He put his arm around her and drew her close. "Maybe we shouldn't leave," he said. "Shame to waste this place, just when it's starting to get interesting. This is the perfect venue to celebrate you bein' my girlfriend."

Kyle was Texas and California all rolled into one—

far too potent a combination. "I haven't agreed to be your girlfriend," she said grouchily.

"So this is the place to think about it. Stay with me, Toni. If all you want to do is order room service and watch late-night movies—that's all we'll do. At least you know you can trust me that much by now."

Trust…she didn't trust her own contrary emotions, that was the real problem. But she found herself gazing into Kyle's dark eyes, and she found herself murmuring, "Yes. I'll stay."

## CHAPTER FIFTEEN

ROOM SERVICE at the resort was excellent. Around midnight Toni and Kyle got a yen for scrambled eggs and English muffins. They'd just finished watching a Cary Grant movie, and there was a bit of a lull before a Jimmy Stewart film came on the screen. The eggs and muffins arrived promptly. Toni watched as Kyle gave the bellhop a generous tip. Generosity—chalk up one more good quality.

Kyle brought the food to the king-size bed. They'd propped up a number of pillows for maximum comfort. Chalk up another in favor of the resort—a healthy supply of pillows. Toni's point system was really getting a workout, considering that she was keeping track of Kyle's good qualities at the same time.

The English muffins came with fresh butter and apricot jam. Kyle and Toni polished off the eggs and muffins, and watched Jimmy Stewart. Pretty soon it was almost two in the morning, but Toni wasn't sleepy. She felt keyed up. Unfortunately, she knew the reason why.

"Another movie?" Kyle asked.

"Yes…no. Dammit, Kyle."

"I want to make love to you, too. But if you need to wait…we'll wait."

She took the remote from him and clicked off the television. Now only the bedside lamp was on. The balcony door was slightly open, just enough for the cool ocean breeze to scent the air.

"Dammit, Kyle," Toni said again. Then she pulled him toward her and kissed him.

They lay among the pillows, taking their time as they touched and held each other. Kyle slowly unbuttoned Toni's blouse. Just as leisurely she unbuttoned his shirt.

"Kyle," she whispered at last. "I like doing everything, but…"

"This time I brought something, Toni."

She gazed into his eyes. "You thought this would happen tonight?"

"I hoped."

"Nothing like being prepared," she said, feeling awkward all of a sudden. But he kissed her some more, and one by one her other items of clothing came off. Bra…underpants…socks last of all. Her toes were sandy from the beach.

"I could look at you all the time," Kyle murmured as he caressed her.

"I could look at you, too." She tugged at his jeans, impatient now. All his clothes came off, too. Heat gathered deep inside Toni. She touched Kyle, experimenting. His low moan of desire rewarded her. But then it was his turn to touch, and all too quickly she found herself spiraling toward loss of control.

"Kyle...you said you brought something..."

"There's still time," he murmured. "Just let go."

As he touched her and kissed her, she did let go, gasping with the pleasure he gave her. Only afterward did he reach across the bed to his jeans and pull out a condom packet. He tore open the packet, and Toni found herself very absorbed in the task of helping him to put the condom on.

"Now, Kyle," she whispered.

Gazing into her eyes, he entered her slowly. But she could tell that neither one of them wanted slow anymore. She arched against him, trying to push him past the edge of control.

"Toni..."

"Yes, Kyle," she said.

They moved together, faster and faster, clinging to each other. Toni was amazed at how quickly her desire had built once more, spinning her out to that place where only sensation existed...

Their cries mingled. And afterward they remained tangled together, as if they were both reluctant to break the contact between them. Toni was damp and hot, the air from the balcony wafting over her with welcome coolness.

"Oh, no," she whispered after a long moment. "With the balcony door open...we made a lot of noise...what if someone heard us?"

Kyle laughed softly and gathered her yet closer. "What if they did?"

"I don't know." She wasn't used to such abandon.

"Toni...you're not going to run away from me, are you?"

She tried to relax again in his arms. "No. Not this time."

"Why do I have the feeling that if we go to sleep, you won't be here in the morning?"

"That's silly," she said. "Of course I'll be here."

He kissed her nose and released her. "We'll see."

Somehow she found his doubts exasperating. "What do you think I'm going to do—grab your convertible and drive off?"

"Toni, practically the minute we stopped making love I could feel you retreat from me."

She didn't want to admit it. "I'm staying, Kyle. I'm not going anywhere."

"It might be nice to wake up together in the morning."

She reached over and switched off the light. "I'll be here. Good *night*, Kyle."

"Good night, Antonia."

She lay still for a long while, wondering if he'd

gone to sleep. He certainly seemed to be breathing
evenly. At last she could no longer contain herself.

"Kyle," she said.

"Yes, Toni."

"I'll agree to it," she said.

"Agree to what?" he asked.

"You know. I'll be your...girlfriend." There. She'd
said it. Had it been so difficult?

"I'm glad, Antonia."

"Doesn't that convince you I'll be here in the morning?" she asked.

"Good night, Antonia."

She lay still for another long while. It did seem to
her that Kyle slept. But she remained awake, listening
to the apprehensive beating of her own heart.

SOMETIME IN THE EARLY HOURS of morning, Toni fell
asleep in spite of herself. When she woke, full sunlight
was already streaming into the room. Kyle slept on,
limbs stretched out comfortably. She gazed at him,
wondering how any man could be so handsome in his
sleep. She saw his rumpled hair, the stubble of beard
along his jaw...and she felt a stirring of the desire that
had already carried her away so impetuously. If Kyle
were to awake right now, at this very moment—she
didn't think she could be held responsible for further
actions.

She had an almost overwhelming urge to poke him.

But then, resisting temptation, she slid out of bed, grabbed her blouse and tiptoed into the bathroom. Although she had not come prepared for an overnight stay, the resort had provided toothbrushes and other amenities. Toni brushed her teeth, washed her face, combed her hair. But when she looked in the mirror, she saw that her skin still seemed flushed from the time she'd spent in Kyle's arms.

"For goodness' sake," she muttered. "Get a grip." She opened the bathroom door and tiptoed into the bedroom again. Kyle was sitting propped up against the pillows, hands clasped behind his head. The sheet rested casually at his waist. He looked...magnificent.

He smiled at Toni. "You're still here."

"Told you I would be," she said, drawing her blouse around her. It afforded little protection, barely skimming her thighs. She glanced around rather desperately for the rest of her clothes.

"Coming back to bed?" Kyle murmured.

"No..."

He waited. And at last, with a mumbled curse, she slid under the covers again. Fortunately, being kingsize, it was a large bed, and she had some distance from Kyle.

"I only came back in because I can't find my clothes, " she said.

"Let's see..." He searched under the sheet, and

produced her bra. She reached over and snatched it from him.

"That's enough," she said. "I'll look for the rest later."

He rolled over on his side and propped his head in his hand. "Do you really need your clothes?" he asked.

"Kyle..."

"You seem tense, Antonia. Awfully tense."

She pulled the sheet up to her chin, feeling more ridiculous by the minute. "I'm just not used to this," she said. "If you want to know the truth, I've never...woken up with a man before."

He seemed interested. "Let me get this straight. You were engaged to be married, but you never woke up with the guy."

She wished her skin wouldn't keep flushing. And she wished she didn't feel obliged to explain. "Greg would spend part of the night with me—but then he'd leave before morning. He said to get ready for work and everything, he had to go to his own place."

"Hmm, and I thought you were the one who had a habit of running away before morning."

"Not in the least," she said. "I would have been perfectly happy for Greg to keep some things at my apartment."

"What did you think was going to happen when the two of you got married?" Kyle asked. "Miraculous transformation—suddenly the guy's ready to share closet space?''

Toni shifted uncomfortably. ''I did assume that once we were married things *would* be different. Marriage is supposed to change things, after all.''

''Nah,'' Kyle said. ''If a guy's a jerk before the wedding vows, he's pretty much a jerk afterward, too. Surprising how few women realize that.''

''Well, I figured it out in time,'' she said.

''Never trust a guy who doesn't stick around until morning,'' Kyle advised.

''You may have a point.''

''Toni, you're going to fall off the bed if you don't watch out.''

She moved a little more toward the center.

''So…are you still my girlfriend?'' he murmured in a way that sent a warm little quiver all down her spine.

''Yes,'' she said.

''Scares the hell out of you, doesn't it?''

''Yes,'' she said.

''But you're sticking around.''

''Yes,'' she said. Then she saw the humor glimmering in his eyes. ''Dammit, Kyle, if you're not going to be serious about this—''

''Oh, I'm serious, all right. I seriously want you to come closer.''

She stayed where she was. ''You're doing it again, Kyle. You got our relationship to a…a certain level, but now you're backing off again. Making a joke out of everything."

"No joke," he said. "The way I look at it, Toni, you and I...we're going steady."

The man was exasperating. "Very funny," she said.

"I mean it. I see us as being exclusive. I hope you see it the same way, too."

"If you're asking me whether or not I plan to see Dan again, the answer is no," she said. "I told you we agreed not to date anymore."

"But it scared the hell out of you, didn't it?" Kyle asked again. "Giving up good old Dan. The guy was a real convenience."

Toni felt very annoyed. "Kyle, I've never used anyone as a *convenience*."

"Sure you have. We all do, at one time or another."

Toni thought it over. "Something just occurred to me, Kyle. All those women Hollan set you up with. Maybe they've been a convenience, too. A way to avoid a real relationship. You can just go around saying what a string of bad luck you've had, without making any effort to find a woman who *wouldn't* be bad luck."

Kyle looked disgruntled. "You're carrying the idea a little too far."

She could tell that she'd hit close to the mark. Somehow that helped her to relax. She arranged the pillows more comfortably and propped herself against them.

"Here's the way I look at it," she said. "Hollan, without meaning to, probably lines you up with a certain type of woman. High-rev, let's call her."

"High-rev," Kyle repeated dubiously.

"Exactly." Toni was almost beginning to enjoy herself. "You know how it is when you punch the gas in a car, and you rev the engine too high? That's the kind of woman I'm talking about. She's revved too high. She has a million concerns, and they're all about *her*. She has a life in utter chaos, and she expects *you* to help fix it. She's utterly fascinated by herself, and she expects *you* to be, too. How am I doing?"

"Lord," Kyle said, "you're right on."

"I thought so," Toni said with satisfaction. But the satisfaction faded at Kyle's next words.

"What you've just done," he said, "is describe your own sister. That's the type of woman Hollan is attracted to. Maybe it's the only kind of woman he knows. So that's the kind of woman he introduces me to. And of course, that's the kind that drives me crazy."

Toni sat up a bit. "I didn't mean to say anything derogatory about my sister. I wasn't even thinking about Jackie. I didn't know you were going to make that connection—"

"Toni, I'm not accusing you of disloyalty. I'm just

saying that when it comes to you and your sister...you're the one who shines. You may not believe that, but it's true.''

She gazed into his eyes, and saw the way he gazed back at her. She felt her skin flushing all over again. All her life she'd been convinced she was less of a dazzler than Jackie. But Kyle made her feel exactly the opposite. He made her feel as if *she* could dazzle for once.

''Toni,'' he murmured, ''are you going to stay on that side of the bed forever?''

Her emotions were too contradictory. One minute she wanted to go right into his arms, the next she felt all her fears tumbling down upon her again.

''Uh, Kyle...I'm already late for work. In two years I've never been late. They're probably wondering what happened to me.''

He reached over, took the phone off the bedside table and handed it to her. ''Guess you'd better call,'' he said helpfully.

She dialed the number, fully prepared to inform the office that she'd be in as soon as possible. But, instead, she ended up with some lame excuse about not knowing when or if she'd be in. She hung up the receiver, dismayed at herself.

Kyle grinned, took the phone from her and called room service. ''What'll it be?'' he asked Toni.

"For crying out loud...bagels and cream cheese. And a glass of orange juice."

When room service came, Kyle got into his jeans and answered the door. Again he brought food to bed. Toni was amazed at how ravenous she felt. They polished off breakfast. And then Kyle came over to her side of the bed.

"We have until noon before they kick us out," he said.

"You're not thinking..."

"I'm thinking exactly what you're thinking, Antonia." She'd neglected to button her blouse all the way, and he proceeded to do interesting things in the unbuttoned area. A tingle went all through her.

"Kyle..."

"Don't worry, I'm prepared," he murmured. He took another small packet from his jeans.

"You didn't bring just one? You brought *two?* You really must have been hoping, Kyle."

"I'm still hoping," he said.

She slid down beside him and wrapped her arms around him. The fear hadn't gone away, but her longings were more intense.

Just how intense, she proceeded to show him.

WHAT WITH ONE THING and another, Toni didn't get back to her apartment until that evening. First of all, she and Kyle had barely made it out of the resort by twelve noon. Second of all, they'd taken time getting back to Heritage City. They'd meandered along the coast in Kyle's silver convertible. They'd stopped often to admire the scenery. Not to mention another activity that kept them occupied in the car. Necking. Just like a pair of teenagers, Toni thought.

She didn't know how she'd had the strength to say goodbye to Kyle. But, in the end, she'd insisted that he leave her at her door. She needed some time alone. Her emotions were in a tumult. Was there any way at all to tame them?

She'd scarcely been home five minutes when the phone rang.

"Hello," she said.

"Hello, Antonia," Kyle's voice murmured sexily in her ear.

She closed her eyes. "Kyle..."

"Here I am, driving to San Francisco all by myself, and you could be with me. Too bad you aren't."

"You know that I have to show up for work tomorrow," she told him.

"It's a shame how real life gets in the way," he said.

"I think you really do have too much time on your hands," she said. "You need to solve your career crisis so you can go back to being a workaholic."

"Wouldn't it be more fun if we just took off together?'' Kyle asked. "We could do some island hopping."

"No islands," Toni said firmly. And then, reluctantly, "Good night, Kyle."

"Good night, Antonia."

She put the phone down. Only a minute or so later it rang again. She couldn't help smiling as she grabbed the receiver.

"Kyle, just because we're going steady is no reason to—"

"Going steady?" came Jackie's incredulous voice. "Now you and Kyle are going *steady?*"

The first rule of lawyering is never to assume anything. Toni wished she'd applied it to answering the phone.

"Just a private joke," she said as casually as possible.

"Tell all," Jackie said. "What'd he do, give you his class ring? No—better yet, his fraternity pin."

"I'll have to ask for it next time I see him," Toni said, trying not to sound aggravated.

"So things are really moving along with you and Kyle. Let me see, what's next? Have you started writing his name in notebooks? 'Kyle Brennan' surrounded by little hearts. And *your* name. 'Toni Shaw Brennan.' Or how about 'Mrs. Kyle Brennan.' More hearts."

"Are you done, Jackie?"

"No. This is too much fun," Jackie said. "My big sister's going steady."

"You did have a reason to call, didn't you?" Toni asked pointedly.

"Right, right. I want to know if you and Kyle have decided on a honeymoon yet."

Kyle and Toni had, indeed, decided that the resort near Carmel would be perfect for Jackie and Hollan. But they'd also agreed not to say anything just yet.

"It's going to be a surprise," Toni informed her sister. "If we tell you now, you and Hollan will only have another excuse to start bickering. Kyle and I are going to make darn sure this honeymoon is worth all the trouble."

"Trouble…you're going *steady* with the man. How much trouble is that?"

Plenty, Toni informed herself silently. Out loud she said, "You've already had your fun, Jackie."

"Not nearly enough. Wow…going steady. Major stuff. Big commitment. The two of you could always carve your initials in a tree. And you could wear a locket with two little pictures of yourselves. Or better yet—"

Toni didn't wait to hear the next suggestion. "Good*bye*," she told her sister, and then she plunked down the receiver.

TONI SAT across from Sarah Martin. She reached into her briefcase, took out a photograph, and placed it on the table. It was the picture in the ivory frame that showed Sarah and a teenage boy ready for the prom.

"Tell me about this night," Toni said gently.

At first Sarah only glanced at the photo with disinterest. She had grown noticeably thinner and paler over the past few weeks. Her light brown hair hung listlessly around her face. Today she hadn't even bothered to pull it back in a ponytail.

"Tell me about Richard," Toni said.

Sarah picked up the photograph and looked it over. "I'd been wanting Richard to ask me to the prom. And when he finally did, I just couldn't believe it." She sounded indifferent, as if recalling a story that had happened to someone else. She stared at the photo. "I looked and looked for a dress," she said in her stony voice. "My mother promised I could have any dress I wanted, but I couldn't find the right one."

"It's a beautiful dress, Sarah. And you looked very pretty in it."

"Sure. You'd say anything to get me to talk." Sarah's mouth twisted in a humorless smile. "I'm talking, aren't I? So I went to the prom with Richard. We had a good time. He brought me home and then...it was over." Sarah pushed the photograph back across the table.

Toni picked it up and studied the uncertain young

teenage boy staring at the camera. "Richard is the father of your child," she said.

"Yes…he's the father," Sarah said automatically. "But he moved away a long time ago and I don't know where he is. I don't care."

Toni had been trying to locate Richard Johnston. He'd left home at seventeen after a falling-out with his widowed father. Like too many teenage runaways, he seemed simply to have disappeared.

Sarah stood, making it clear that she no longer wished to talk. But, just before the guard led her away, she looked back at Toni.

"I killed my baby," she said, her voice still expressionless. "It doesn't matter how it happened. I'm the one who killed him. And now that he's gone…I wish I was gone, too."

## CHAPTER SIXTEEN

THREE DAYS LATER, Toni drove through the wine country in her hatchback. She knew the trip would be a lot more enjoyable in Kyle's silver convertible. But, even though she was meeting him up here, she'd insisted on coming in her own car. It had seemed important to maintain a little distance.

The gold and crimson of the autumn vineyards had only deepened, and the scent of harvested grapes still hung upon the air. Toni slowed as she turned onto the narrow road leading to her grandfather's land. She went through an apple orchard and past old farmhouses and crumbling barns. When she came to the rutted track at the edge of the wildflower meadow, she saw the convertible already parked. She got out of her car, went across the meadow and climbed the hillside through the oaks. After a few moments she came out upon the grassy verge where Kyle stood.

"Hello," she said awkwardly.

"Hello, Toni." He looked her over. "Funny thing," he said lightly. "I have a girlfriend, but she's been avoiding me. Keeps saying she can't see me, gets off the phone in a hurry every time I call.''

Toni tried to give a nonchalant shrug, knowing right away that she was unsuccessful at it. "Kyle, I already told you. I've been awfully busy. I've spent so much time on the Martin case that I've fallen behind on my other cases. I've been trying to catch up.''

He didn't look convinced, but he played along. "How is the Martin case going?" he asked.

"Worse than ever. My client now out and out says that she killed her baby. It doesn't help my defense.''

"Do you believe her?" Kyle asked.

"I don't know what to believe anymore." She paused. "Yesterday I had that meeting with the three big guys...Allingdale, Reed and Mathews.''

"How'd it go?''

"I was a little nervous at first, but then I actually began to feel comfortable. No offer yet, but they said they'd be making a decision very soon.''

Kyle nodded gravely. "So you were in San Francisco yesterday, but you didn't think the two of us should get together. Even for a quick lunch, that type of thing.''

"Kyle, I told you. I was busy." She took a deep breath. "I don't know why you're making a big deal out of this. It's only been a few days since we were at that resort.''

"I don't want to take over your life, Toni. I've already told you I like the idea of two people who have separate pursuits as well as a common ground. The separate pursuits, we have that covered. The common ground...I don't think so. We got too close, as far as you were concerned, and you started to run again.''

She stuffed her hands into the pockets of her coat. The late-afternoon air seemed to carry a chill. ''I'm not running away. I'm sure we can arrange a date for this weekend. I certainly have my Saturday nights free.''

Kyle didn't say anything. Perhaps her lack of enthusiasm had overwhelmed him. She wished she could explain to him what she was feeling right now. Part of her wanted to spend every possible moment in his arms. The other part was terrified of needing him too much.

''I'm glad you asked me up here,'' she said. ''I was hoping you'd finally show me the designs for the house.''

''Right.'' He bent down and picked up a long cardboard tube, easing some rolled-up sheets of drafting paper from it. ''I decided I couldn't show you these unless we were actually on location,'' he said.

''I'm glad,'' she repeated. ''I mean...I like coming up here. And being here...with you.'' She cursed herself. She realized that now she was trying too hard, and Kyle wasn't falling for it. He'd grown somewhat reserved. He unrolled the house plans and displayed them for her perusal as if she were simply another client.

At first Toni examined a few exterior sketches of the house. She saw the curved wall of glass, now fitted charmingly into the overall plan: a two-story home with clean, modern lines yet an appealing hint of the old-fashioned in all the curved edges. One of the more distinctive touches was a grooved frieze that ran all along the edge of the roof, unifying the entire design. Toni traced it with a finger.

"It's the funniest thing," she murmured. "What you've done reminds me of something about Grandpa. He had a china plate that he was very fond of, the only remnant of a set he and Grandma bought when they were first married. In the years after she died, all the china seemed to break at different times until Grandpa had only the one plate left. He decided he'd better take extra-special care of it. It was a creamy white with a blue pattern all around the edge. And somehow...well, somehow the house you've drawn reminds me of Grandpa washing and drying that china plate with all the care possible. And...that makes me feel good."

"I'm willing to bet you're the one who has the plate now," Kyle said.

"As a matter of fact I do. I keep it wrapped up and put away because now I feel like it's *my* job to keep it safe. Kyle…how did you manage to design a house that reminds me of Grandpa?''

''I was just designing something for you, Toni. But you haven't seen the rest of it.''

He showed her one layout after another. There was a sunroom that incorporated the lovely curved wall of glass, an intimate dining nook that opened onto a garden, a den that looked cozy enough for snuggling and watching old movies…

Toni decided that she was letting her imagination run away with her. She was relieved when Kyle began walking around the grassy verge, showing her just where everything would be located.

''The sunroom would face this way,'' he said, ''and over behind there—that will be the perfect place for the greenhouse…here's the front patio…''

Toni walked with him. The house came to life for her, room by room. She'd already been able to tell from Kyle's sketches that he'd captured her love of light and spare, simple lines. How had he done it? How had he been able to see inside her so well?

They came full circle and sat down in the overgrown grass. Kyle began to roll up the designs.

''No,'' Toni said. ''Not just yet.'' She had to peruse the sketches again. A new longing engulfed her now, a yearning for a real home. It was a home that she hadn't known existed until today.

At last she rolled up the designs and handed them

back to Kyle. "They're beautiful," she told him. "All I can say is...thank you, Kyle. I think Grandpa would have liked this house very much, and that means a lot to me."

Kyle eased the designs back into the cardboard tube. "You really loved your grandfather, didn't you?"

"Like I always used to tell him...bunches."

Kyle seemed to be puzzling something over, but then he spoke. "Maybe I'm talking out of turn, but your father seems to think that your grandfather was a dissatisfied man. He wants to make sure that he's different."

She drew her legs up, wrapped her arms around them. "Dad and Grandpa never got along that well," she admitted. "Grandpa was a homebody, content to run a shoe store in Heritage till he retired. He liked his customers, and he liked telling stories to anyone who'd listen. Dad didn't want to listen. He wanted to go off and live his own stories. But he has it wrong if he thinks Grandpa was dissatisfied. One of the last things Grandpa ever told me was that he'd had a good life. His only regret was that he and his son just seemed to rub each other the wrong way."

"Families," Kyle remarked.

"Yes...families," Toni agreed. "I wouldn't give mine up, though." She glanced around. "And I think Grandpa would have liked to see your house on his land."

Kyle regarded her quizzically. "The house is still just on paper. You made it clear you didn't want to see it built."

"I suppose you're asking me if I've changed my mind. Frankly, I'd love to see the house built. Someday. But right now I think perhaps it should remain on paper."

"Toni, that's what's known as a nonanswer. You didn't say yes, and you didn't say no."

She put her briefcase in her lap and began unbuckling it. "Right now I'm between yes and no." She took out some candy bars and handed him one. "This time I'm the one who brought the snacks."

He peeled off a wrapper. "I thought you said we couldn't live off candy bars."

"Did I say that? I suppose they're fine as an occasional indulgence." Lately, when it came to Kyle, she'd been indulging...more than occasionally. Her gaze traveled over him. The truth be known, she'd missed him this past week. It had taken all her willpower to stay away from him, and to try imposing discipline on her wayward thoughts. But now he was here, right in front of her, and she couldn't resist.

"Oh, damn, Kyle," she said. She moved closer to him and raised her face for his kiss.

"You taste like chocolate," he murmured a long moment later.

"So do you." She felt warm inside, warm and chocolaty. "Maybe this boyfriend–girlfriend thing is going to work out, after all," she said.

His eyes were dark as he gazed at her. "Maybe you think it'll work out as long as you confine me to Wednesdays and Saturdays."

She didn't think Kyle Brennan was the type of man who could be confined. "That's not exactly how I see it," she said. "I'm willing to work on the common-ground part."

"Are you?" He paused for a long moment. "Then marry me, Toni."

She figured they'd been through this before. "Sure. We do a little role-playing. We've already figured out our engagement. This time we can project to our twentieth wedding anniversary. Or make it our thirtieth—"

"Marry me," he repeated.

She stared at him. He seemed completely serious, all humor vanished for once.

"Kyle, something tells me this isn't a joke."

"No joke. I want us to get married."

She tried some futile humor of her own. "Don't you think you're being a bit precipitous? After all, I just agreed to be your girlfriend. According to Jackie, that means we haven't even made it to the sock hop yet…"

"Toni, will you marry me?"

According to her calculations, this was the fourth time he'd asked in about as many minutes. But that was her fault, not his. Her heart was pounding, and she set down her candy bar without eating any more.

"I heard you the first time," she said. "Let's back up, Kyle. This is moving way too fast."

He stood, and paced restlessly in front of her. "I don't see why," he said. "Toni, all along you've accused me of holding back. Hedging my bets. Refusing to put my money where my mouth was."

"I don't recall telling you that last one—"

He took her hand and drew her up beside him. "Hell, Toni. I want to be with you. I have a feeling you want to be with me, too, if only you'd stop being afraid. Marry me. I'll build this house for you. We'll have a family that will cause us no end of grief, but that's what families are for. Marry me, Toni. I have a suspicion we were meant to be together, you and I."

"No, Kyle," she whispered, pulling away from him. "I can't do it. I just can't. Please don't ask—"

"But I *am* asking. I've stopped holding back, and I think it's time for you to stop holding back, too. Let's not throw away the chance we have."

"I can't do it," she repeated, her voice bleak.

He regarded her for a long moment, his expression very serious. The humor was definitely gone. "Maybe you gave up Dan Greene too soon," he said. And, after that, he tucked the cardboard tube under his arm and walked down the hill...away from Toni.

JACKIE WAS STRETCHED OUT on a table, a towel draped over her and spinach leaves covering her eyes.

"Let me get this straight," she said to Toni. "Kyle Brennan proposed, and you turned him down."

Toni lay on an adjoining table, spinach leaves damp and cool against her own eyes. Her sister had invited her to spend the afternoon at the Never-Too-Late Day Spa in San Francisco. Colorful signs plastered all over the walls admonished, It's Never Too Late—To Get In Shape!

"Kyle did ask me to marry him," she said. "Several times, if you really want to get technical about it. And I did say no." She tried to sound nonchalant, but the cold hard ache inside her wouldn't go away.

"Tell me again why you said no," Jackie instructed. "I want to make sure I have this straight."

"I have several reasons," Toni said. "The last time someone proposed to me it ended in total disaster."

"I don't buy it," Jackie said. "Kyle isn't thinks-he's-so-cool-but-he's-really-a-jackass Greg. Next reason."

"It was all moving too fast," Toni said. "I'd barely agreed to be his girlfriend, and suddenly he has us in a house with two-point-five children."

"I don't buy that one, either," said Jackie. "Look at *me*. *I'm* starting a family. You don't see *me* hyperventilating, do you?"

"Actually—"

"Next," Jackie said imperiously.

Toni hesitated. She hadn't even mentioned this reason yet, but she supposed it couldn't be avoided. "He didn't say he loved me."

"Uh-oh. This time you may have something."

Before the conversation could proceed any further, an attendant came into the room and peeled away the spinach. The woman peered at Toni, then shook her head as if the spinach had been a complete failure.

"Maybe next time we should try the endive," Toni said.

The attendant didn't so much as crack a smile. "Footbath time," she said.

Before Toni knew it, both she and Jackie were sitting with their feet immersed in something that looked like purple slush. Granted, it felt remarkably soothing.

"Okay," Jackie said as soon as they were alone again. "He didn't say he loved you. But maybe you missed something. Maybe he said it, but not in so many words."

Toni replayed the proposal in her mind, and the cold weight inside her only grew heavier. It didn't matter how good her feet felt, her heart ached.

"Let's see," she said. "He told me that he wants to be with me, and that he thinks we were meant to be together."

"Promising," said Jackie, "but doesn't really do the job. Are you sure there wasn't something else?"

"Nothing that can be construed as 'I love you.'"

Jackie shook her head almost sorrowfully. "Afraid you do have a problem here, sis. I mean, no matter what Hollan and I go through, he always ends up telling me how incredibly *much* he loves me."

Toni hadn't thought there'd ever be a time she'd envy Jackie and Hollan. "Maybe it wouldn't have made any difference," Toni speculated. "Maybe he could have said the words, and I still would have been terrified. Just because a man says he loves you…doesn't mean he'll be saying it fifty years down the road."

"My, we are looking ahead, aren't we?" Jackie said. "But there's a solution, you know. You could always tell *Kyle* you love him, and then see what happens."

Toni moved her feet in the purple slush. "No. I can't do that. I can't possibly."

"Why not?" Jackie demanded.

"Because I don't know if I love him!"

"You know," Jackie said. "Don't you, Toni?"

Toni stared at the purple slush. "I love him," she said, her voice low. "Oh, I do love him. But don't you see, Jackie? That's what really terrifies me. The fact that I've fallen in love with Kyle Brennan, after all."

JOGGING IN the early-morning fog was one of Kyle's favorite activities. He liked the way the fog swirled around him, changing the landscape into something unrecognizable, something mysterious. Shapes loomed and faded, everything made unfamiliar.

"I hate the damn fog," Hollan said as he ran beside Kyle. "Can't tell if I'm going forward or backward."

"I thought Jackie was what made you feel that way."

"Yeah...Jackie," Hollan said mournfully.

"I know. She drives you crazy," Kyle said.

"Can't live without her. Wondering if I can live *with* her."

Kyle dodged a fire hydrant. Hollan almost bumped into it.

"Damn fog," he said. And then, "Jackie says you and Toni found a honeymoon spot. Says Toni won't tell her where it is. Says I'm supposed to find out from you."

"Divide and conquer, that it?" Kyle said. "Sorry but Toni and I do agree on one thing. For now, the honeymoon's a surprise. Once you tie the knot, you'll find out all about it. By then it'll be too late for either one of you to find something wrong."

"Jackie wants a perfect honeymoon," Hollan said lugubriously.

"Maybe there's no such thing," Kyle said.

"Maybe not."

Toni would probably agree with that. It seemed she

didn't believe in honeymoons and happy-ever-afters. But Kyle had to get at least one thing right in his life.

"Let's talk business," he told Hollan. "I've decided you came up with a damn good idea. We'll keep our partnership, only it'll be different this time. We take on another couple of architects...handpicked. We spread out the work. Maybe that way everybody gets to do the projects that interest them most."

"No kidding," Hollan said, sounding happy. "You're coming back on board."

"Technically, I guess I never left."

"Not really," Hollan said. "What about the Russ Parker job?"

"I'm taking it as part of the new partnership," Kyle said. "It's going to keep me busy for a long time."

"No sweat," Hollan said. "We start interviewing new guys Monday morning."

"It'll be different, " Kyle reminded him. "It won't be just Nash and Brennan Architects anymore."

"So change is good. So I guess your career crisis is over," Hollan said.

"Guess it is." What he was doing felt right. All the pieces seemed to be falling into place, after all. But the emptiness remained. Maybe his career was finally in order, but he couldn't say the same for his personal life. He'd offered Toni Shaw everything he knew how to give, and she'd turned him down.

Where he went from here, he sure as hell didn't know.

# CHAPTER SEVENTEEN

IT WAS LATE AT NIGHT, but Toni had been granted special permission to visit the county jail. She'd heard reports that Sarah Martin was suffering from nightmares. And so perhaps now was the time she'd be most vulnerable—the time when she might confide some small detail that would help Toni.

Sarah's face seemed drained of all color in the light from the overhead bulb. She sat down across from Toni and gave her a sardonic look that seemed much too old for her years.

"Is this some new tactic?" she asked. "Bring your clients out in the dead of night. Maybe they'll finally give in and tell you what virtuous, misunderstood people they really are."

"That's the general idea here," Toni said.

Sarah laughed mirthlessly. "I bet all your clients are just like me, Ms. Shaw. Criminals. Murderers."

"Are you really a murderer, Sarah?"

Something tightened in the young girl's face. "Yes. I am."

"Why don't I believe you?" Toni asked.

"You should believe me. I want to go back to sleep now. Are we finished?"

"The word is that you're not sleeping," Toni said. "Something's waking you up every night, and I have the feeling it's not because you killed your son. Why don't you tell me about your stepfather, Sarah."

"What do you want to know?" the girl asked flippantly. "He's a great guy. Ask anybody."

"I have been asking around. Some people say he's a fine neighbor, an admirable employee. But one of your neighbors finally confessed that Rob Martin makes her uneasy. She says she doesn't like the way he looks at you, Sarah. She says it's not the way a father should look at a daughter."

Sarah flinched, as if Toni had hit her. Toni hated what she was doing, but she saw no choice. Somehow, before it was too late, she had to get through to Sarah Martin.

"There's nothing wrong," Sarah said woodenly. "I get along with my stepdad. Everybody knows that."

"Maybe he gets along too well with you." Toni knew her words were harsh, perhaps even cruel. But she wasn't turning back now. She saw something flicker in Sarah's eyes. "Maybe," she said, "you're afraid to tell people about your stepfather. But you don't have to be afraid to tell me, Sarah. I'll listen."

Sarah's mouth began to tremble. "Nothing's wrong," she repeated in her stony voice. "Nothing."

Toni had always tried to maintain a professional distance with her clients. She knew that objectivity was one of her best tools for defending. But she reached across the table and took the girl's hands in her own. "Sarah, tell me the truth. It's the only thing that will save you. And you're worth saving—trust me."

Sarah's face seemed to crumple. She began to sob—dry, hacking sobs, as if she had long ago forgotten how to cry. Toni brought her chair right next to the girl's and gathered Sarah in her arms.

"It'll be all right," she murmured as if to a small child. "Just tell me what happened. It'll be all right."

Sarah cried for a long time, in a torrent of tears. Her whole body shook, but she let Toni hold her. At last her sobs quieted down. When she lifted her head, Toni saw her red-rimmed eyes and the wet streaks down her cheeks. Even Sarah's drab jail uniform was damp from tears that had been held back too long. But now Sarah was oddly calm.

"It started when I was thirteen," she said. "At first it was just like…an extra hug. But then he'd come into my room at night. And he'd get into bed with me."

Toni felt a deep chill. But Sarah continued to speak calmly, evenly, as if discussing something that had happened to someone else. Maybe that was how she'd survived—distancing herself as far as possible.

"He said not to tell anybody. He said it was our

secret, and if I told, no one would believe me anyway." She paused. "He was always sorry afterward. He kept saying he wouldn't do it again. But he kept coming back to my room."

Toni thought about that cramped, dreary house where the Martins had lived, and the chill inside her only deepened. "Sarah—your mother. Didn't she try to stop it?"

"She didn't know," Sarah said, still in that strangely uninvolved tone. "He worked at a hotel, so he came home late at night. She was always asleep. And when I tried to tell her...she said, 'Sarah, let's go buy something nice for you. Let's only think about nice things.' One time I put the bureau in front of my door. But he got in anyway. And he said never to do that again." The sentences tumbled out, disjointed, but the story was all too terribly clear.

Sarah pressed a hand to her stomach. "I started a baby, and I was really scared. And he said, 'For sure you can't tell anybody now. Who was that boy who took you to the prom? You say he's the father. He's gone anyway. He left town. Everybody'll believe he's the father.' So that's what I said, but I hated the baby inside me. I hated it. But then he didn't come into my room anymore and that's when I knew the baby saved me."

Toni sat completely still. The rest of it poured out

of Sarah—everything that had been held back too long.

"I thought Jeremy for a boy, Jessica for a girl. And then Jeremy was born and I never loved anybody so much. My room was just for me and Jeremy. Nobody else. And I thought, as soon as I can I'll get a job, and a whole house for Jeremy and me. Nobody else. But then one night he came back to my room. And I yelled. I yelled so loud she had to hear. And I said, 'Never come to my room again.'" Sarah took a quavering breath and bent her head. All the words seemed to have drained out of her.

Toni wished she could let Sarah rest now. And yet, for Sarah's sake, they had to continue. No words could be left unspoken tonight.

"Sarah," Toni said gently. "Tell me about the day Jeremy died."

"No," Sarah whispered. "No."

"You have to tell me." Toni kept her voice steady and firm. "Tell me, and then it will be over."

"It will never be over," Sarah said, her own voice shaking. "And I already told you! He came into my room and I yelled. Because of Jeremy I was strong and I yelled. And then Mom was there and she said, 'No, it can't be true,' but I wouldn't lie anymore. And the very next day I went and I looked for a job. All day I looked, but I didn't find one. I came home and I heard Jeremy crying…crying so hard. I went into my room and Mom was shaking him. Over and over, she was shaking him, and screaming at him. 'Why?' she said. 'Why are you here?' And then she saw me, and she dropped Jeremy and she ran away. I took Jeremy in my arms and held him, and he stopped crying. And then he stopped breathing.'' Sarah raised her head, and now fresh tears trickled down her cheeks. "I held him while he died. And it was all my fault, don't you see? Because I made her listen to me. If I'd kept quiet, he wouldn't have died. I know it. So I killed him. I'm the one who killed him.''

Once again Toni took both Sarah's hands in her own and held them tight. "You didn't kill him, Sarah. You didn't.''

But Sarah only sat there with the tears streaming down her cheeks, crying for the baby she had lost.

TONI WAS SO UPSET after her encounter with Sarah Martin that she drove around all night. By the early hours of morning she knew she needed to get some sleep, but she just couldn't bear to go home. She drove to her parents' house and let herself in the door. She moved silently, in case nobody was up yet. Tiptoeing to the living room, she set down her briefcase and curled up on the sofa, where she'd spent many childhood hours—listening to her parents read stories, playing and quarreling with her sister, sharing all the ups and downs of a family. Not a perfect family…just a good family.

Just then, Marianne Shaw padded into the room in her slippers, belting her bathrobe as she came. "Honey," she said in concern, "are you okay?"

Toni straightened. "Hi, Mom. Sorry…I just had to be here for a little while. No need to go into the details right now. A rough case, that's all."

Marianne sat down beside her and patted her hand. "I'm glad you're here. Any hour of the day or night, you know that."

Toni gave a tired smile. "Yes, I know. I guess I wanted to tell you…thanks for being my mother. Watching out for me, and making sure no one ever hurt me. I don't think I've ever really thanked you for that."

Marianne peered at her, giving her another concerned look. "It's not like you to get sentimental, dear. Are you sure you're all right? And I haven't been the perfect mother, Toni…I've always felt guilty about something. The way I let Jackie have so much of my attention. I know you've felt left out a lot of times."

"Oh, Mom," Toni said with tears in her eyes.

"Honey." Now Marianne squeezed her hand. "It doesn't change the fact that Jackie tends to take over, and I tend to let her."

"I let her do it, too," Toni said. "And you know

what? We'll probably keep letting her do it. Because she loves us as much as we love her.''

"You *are* sentimental," Marianne said.

"Yes, I guess I am." Toni patted her cheeks with a tissue and at the same time stifled a yawn. "I'm also asleep on my feet. I'm going home to crash, before I wake up Dad, too."

"Your father isn't here," Marianne said, glancing away.

Now Toni was the one who gave a look of concern. "Where is he, Mom? Oh, Lord, he didn't move out, did he? I know the two of you are having problems, but still—"

"Don't get dramatic, on top of everything else," Marianne chided. "No, your father did not move out. He went on a camping trip yesterday, and he won't be back for at least a few days. He said he was going stir-crazy. He said something about needing to go find some real fish for once. Fine, I told him. You need to travel—by all means, travel. Get started right away. Don't let me stop you."

"Oh, Mom…"

"I don't want you to worry about it. If your father and I parted in a bit of a huff—these things happen." But Marianne looked unhappy.

The front door opened and closed.

"Don't tell me," Marianne said. "Your sister had

a sixth sense we were meeting without her, and she couldn't bear the thought…Jackie, is that you?''

Toni's father appeared in the doorway, wearing his fishing cap and his thermal vest. He didn't seem surprised to see Toni at this unearthly hour. ''It's me,'' he said gruffly.

Marianne stood, belting her bathrobe all over again. She seemed nervous. ''Charles, what are you doing back so soon?''

''What do you think?'' he grumbled. ''I got lonely. I missed you. And I decided—heck, if you don't want to travel, we won't travel. I'd rather stay planted right here than have you miserable. Who needs Switzerland? Who needs China…Australia?''

''Oh, honey.'' Marianne went straight into her husband's arms. The two of them stood very close, their arms wrapped around each other. Toni watched her parents in fascination.

''I mean it,'' said Charles. ''I'd rather have you than all the adventures in the world.''

''Goodness gracious, now stop with the martyr routine,'' Marianne said. ''You're going to have me *and* adventures.''

''But what about this doctorate of yours—''

''Just let me finish,'' said Marianne. ''I'm going back to school, and you're going off on adventures. You'll send me lots of postcards and I'll run up an outrageous phone bill.''

"I don't want to travel without you," Charles said grumpily.

"A lot of the time we'll travel together—summers and Christmas vacations. The rest of the time, you'll follow your own adventures. Who knows, you might even get tired of traveling three hundred and sixty-five days a year. Maybe you'll only want to do it two hundred days a year. But you have to find that out for yourself, honey. We both have to go after what we've been missing."

These words sounded suspiciously like what Kyle had tried to tell Toni. Two people really could love each other for years and years, and somehow manage to work out their differences.

Now she picked up her briefcase and edged toward the door. She figured her parents could use some quality time alone, but her father wasn't going to let her off so easily.

"Fine fellow, that Kyle Brennan," he said pointedly, just before Toni slipped out the door.

IT WAS A WEEK before Jackie's wedding and her cable station was throwing her a big prewedding bash. No expense had been spared. It seemed an entire hotel in downtown San Francisco had been taken over for the occasion. There was a caterer and a band, not to mention balloons and streamers in every color of the rainbow. As far as Toni could tell, it all pointed to the fact that Jackie's employers valued her a great deal. Why couldn't Jackie see that, for once?

At the moment, Jackie was dancing in the center of the floor with Hollan. The two of them gazed moonily at each other in between executing several impressive steps. Now and then a smattering of applause surrounded them. Toni had a feeling that Jackie and Hollan would manage to find the center of attention wherever they went.

Kyle was dancing, too, with a very well-toned brunette. The two of them didn't do any fancy moves, but they looked good out there on the floor. Toni wondered dourly if the brunette spent a lot of time at places like the Never-Too-Late Spa. The song ended and Kyle escorted the brunette to her seat. Then he came over to Toni's table.

"Hello," he said. He was far too handsome in that smoky-gray jacket. It made his hair look richer and darker than ever.

"Hello," she said. "Having fun?"

Without waiting for an invitation, he sat down next to her. "What you'd really like to believe," he said, "is that a mere two weeks after proposing to you— and being rejected—I'm out and about on the town with a new lady friend. That way you could think I'm just as lousy as your ex-fiancé, Greg."

She wished that the heavy ache inside her would go

away. Instead, it seemed to have lodged permanently in the area of her heart.

"It's no business of mine," she said, "who you go out and about with."

"Hate to disappoint you," Kyle said. "She's the happily married wife of a former client. She tells me that if I ever meet the right girl, she'll invite the two of us over to her house for a barbecue."

Toni knew only one thing. If this very minute Kyle were to say he loved her, she'd fling her arms around him and never let go. She waited. They looked at each other.

"Congratulations," Toni murmured at last. "Jackie tells me that you and Hollan are partners again."

"When you've been friends as long as we have, I guess partnership is inevitable. I took the Russ Parker job, by the way. I'm already working on the designs."

She heard the enthusiasm in his voice. "I'm glad, Kyle," she said sincerely. "Very glad. I think you'll have a grand time."

He propped his elbows on the table. "It won't be easy, keeping the isolated atmosphere of the surroundings yet still building a resort there. I think it can be managed, though."

"I'm glad," she repeated, even as she tried not to think about the island.

"How about you, Toni? Any offers lately from Allingdale, Reed and Mathews?"

She took a sip of her wine, but scarcely tasted it. "A very magnanimous offer," she said. "All the perks and benefits you could ever want, on a partnership track, no less. Can you believe I'd turn something like that down?"

He studied her. "I can believe it."

"Well, I did turn it down. Toni Shaw, overworked, underpaid public defender—that's me. I guess I figure that if there's even one more Sarah Martin out there who needs me...I'll be around."

"The Martin case," Kyle said. "How'd that turn out?"

She swirled the wine in her glass. "Maybe I'll share the details with you someday. Sarah didn't kill her own child, but she's going to have a very difficult time ahead. Factor in years of heavy-duty counseling, just for starters. Somehow she has to find a life for herself. I'll keep tabs on her, for what it's worth."

"It's probably worth a lot," Kyle said.

They didn't seem to have much else to say. Toni felt a tightness in her throat that made speaking difficult.

"Well," she managed to say at last, "I'm glad everything's working out for you, Kyle."

"Not everything."

*Tell me you love me*, she pleaded silently. *Just tell me that, and somehow I'll get over the fears.*

He didn't tell her. Yet she had to go on, attempting a semblance of normalcy.

"I guess we have everything wrapped up for Jackie and Hollan's honeymoon," she said. "I made the reservations."

"I arranged for the limo," Kyle said.

"Nice touch, a limo. Jackie will appreciate it. Well...nothing more to do I suppose."

He gazed at her. "No. Nothing more."

She thought she'd known about heartbreak before, with Greg. But she'd been wrong. She hadn't truly discovered heartbreak until Kyle Brennan came into her life.

## CHAPTER EIGHTEEN

IT WASN'T ALL that difficult to find an ex-fiancé when you needed one, particularly if the ex-fiancé had a habit of walking his large black Labrador every evening. Toni watched as Greg came down the street, the dog, as usual, pulling at the leash. When the Lab saw Toni, he bounded forward and nearly bowled her over. He wagged his tail in delight.

"Hey, old friend," said Toni, giving the dog a good rub on the head. "Hey, Skip. You remember me, don't you? Sure you do."

"Toni." Greg stood at the other end of the leash. "Fancy seeing you here," he said, his tone too casual.

Toni gave the dog another pet, and then perused her ex-fiancé. She noted all the reasons she'd been attracted to him in the first place: brown hair worn fashionably long, blue eyes behind wire-frame glasses, unassuming demeanor, lanky build. It all combined into a man easy to gaze upon. At least, Toni told herself, she hadn't had poor judgment about Greg when it came to the looks department. There'd also been a time when looking at him had sent a flutter through her. No flutter today.

"Either you ran into me on purpose," Greg said, "or we're fated to see each other again. Something tells me it's not fate."

Greg had always tried too hard to be witty. As if he believed that if he kept laying it on, people would ignore his lapses in good behavior. Little lapses, such as sleeping around on his fiancée.

"You can relax," Toni said. "I'm not here for a reconciliation."

"Didn't think so," Greg said. "Not after the way you said goodbye to me last time. Basically, you told me to go to hell."

Maybe this was going to be more difficult than Toni had anticipated, but it had to be done. "Mind if I walk with the two of you for a while?" she said.

"Sure. Why not. Old times' sake." Now he sounded a bit forced. Skip was already straining at the leash again, and they went on down the street. "How've you been, Toni?" Greg asked. "I mean... really."

"Are you asking if I've been crying into my pillow every night over you?"

He gave a laugh that was too jocular. "Always direct. That's you, Toni. I guess I'm supposed to tell you what an ass I was."

"Funny, that's just what Jackie calls you."

"No love lost on this end, either," Greg said.

"In answer to your question," she said, "I've been fine. How about you?"

"Not seeing anybody right now," he said. "Maybe that surprises you, but it's the truth."

"I didn't come by to talk about your love life, Greg."

"No kidding. Thought you'd want to hear every detail." Greg didn't have to spell it out any further— he was on the defensive.

Skip tugged on the leash, and it seemed they all had to walk a little faster. One of the things that had first drawn Toni to Greg was his affection for his dog. Only later had she come to realize that Skip served a purpose, too. For example, it was always justifiable to say you couldn't stay at your fiancée's apartment too long because you had to get home to the dog.

"You're obviously here for a reason, Toni," Greg said. "Shall we cut to it?"

"I'm definitely not here because I want to get back together, or anything frightening like that."

"I wouldn't be frightened," he said. "I'd be surprised."

"I'm sure. Anyway, Greg, I'm here because…" She tried to think of a good way to say it. *I'm here because I needed to see you again, to figure out if I have any unresolved feelings. And you know what? No feelings. Not a one.*

Toni felt as if a burden had just lifted from her shoulders. She'd been carrying it around these past months, but now it was gone.

"You know why I came, Greg? To say a real goodbye."

"Goodbye…we just said hello."

"Yes, but I think that's enough, don't you? Here, Skip. Here, old boy." She petted the dog one last time. "Happy life," she told him.

"Toni, maybe we could go somewhere," Greg said. "Have a cup of coffee."

"I don't think so," Toni said. "It's not what either one of us wants. Goodbye, Greg." She looked at him one last time. No, not even a flutter. Smiling to herself, feeling that new buoyancy, she walked on down the street.

IT WAS JACKIE AND HOLLAN'S wedding day. The church was overflowing with guests. The bridesmaids and flower girls were milling around in the vestibule. The organ had started to play, the music swelling majestically on the air. There was only one slight problem. Make that two slight problems. The bride hadn't shown. And neither had the groom.

The bride's mother came hurrying up to Kyle and bustled him into the sacristy. "We have to talk where no one can overhear us," said Marianne Shaw with a distracted expression. "We don't want anybody to know yet that the wedding party is minus a few members.''

"I think people are going to figure that out pretty soon," Kyle said.

"This is awful. We all worked so hard to get them this far. And just as they're supposed to march down the aisle, they've vanished. I've heard of the groom not showing up. I've heard of the bride not showing up. But *both* of them?''

With Jackie and Hollan, that really didn't come as much of a surprise. Nonetheless, Kyle thought it best to be tactful with the bride's mother. "I've tried calling every place I can think of," he told her. "No luck.''

"Didn't Hollan say anything to you...anything at all that would give you a clue?" Marianne looked at him hopefully.

"Nothing beyond the usual prenuptial panic," Kyle said. "Let's see, at the wedding rehearsal he only forgot his lines once. And he only had a little too much to drink at the bachelor party.''

"The bachelor party," Marianne muttered darkly. "I didn't even think of that.''

"There weren't any girls jumping out of cakes," Kyle said. "Nothing that could have gotten him too carried away.''

"Well, where *is* the man? And where is my daughter?''

Just then Marianne's other daughter poked her head into the room. "Mom," Toni said. "Someone said you wanted to see me in here—oh." She looked at Kyle and her cheeks turned pink.

"Thank goodness you're here, Toni," said Marianne. "You and Kyle put your heads together and figure out what to do next."

"Why Kyle and me?"

"Because you're the resident experts on Hollan and Jackie. Meanwhile, I'll go out there and try to stall. Let's just hope the organist knows a few good show tunes." As Marianne went out the door, she gave her daughter a nudge, sending Toni into the room to stand before Kyle.

She looked beautiful. She always looked beautiful, but admittedly there was something special about today. With her dark blond hair swept up and strewn with orange blossoms, she looked incredible. The emerald bridesmaid dress draping off her shoulders only contributed to the effect.

Toni seemed to follow the direction of his gaze, and tugged a little at the silk of the dress. "Damn thing," she said.

He wanted to forget all about Jackie and Hollan. Mainly, he wanted to take Toni in his arms and kiss her until she forgot about them, too. The sacristy, however, didn't seem to be the right atmosphere, what with vestments hanging up everywhere.

"I can't imagine where Jackie is," Toni said. "Do you think they had another one of their arguments?"

"It's a safe bet. They're always having one of their arguments," Kyle said. "I think they like arguing. All that drama and then they get to make up."

"But to miss their own wedding…"

"Sounds just like Jackie and Hollan to me. What could grab everybody's attention more than *not* showing?"

"You may have a point." She fiddled with one of the orange blossoms in her hair. "Kyle, I thought I should tell you something," she said. "Yesterday, I…went to see Greg."

He wasn't sure he wanted to hear this, but he listened anyway.

"You gave me the idea," she said. "You suggested maybe I still had feelings for him. So I had to see him to find out if…well, to find out if there was any flame for the old flame." She looked at him. "That was a joke," she said.

He didn't feel like laughing. "Any flame?" he asked.

"Let's put it this way. You could have given me some matches and some kindling, and I still wouldn't have been able to build a fire."

He didn't care if it was the sacristy, after all. He stepped forward and took Toni into his arms. She felt good there, as if she was right where she belonged.

"Now I have something to tell you," he said.

She put her hands against his chest. "Wait. I'm not finished—"

"Afraid this can't wait," he said. "Toni, I love you."

"Damn," she said.

"That wasn't the reaction I was hoping for," he said.

"You stole my thunder, Kyle. Because that's exactly what I was going to tell you. Oh, I love you..."

Several kisses later he allowed her to take a breath, but he went on holding her close. He didn't mind that orange blossoms were tickling his nose.

"Toni," he murmured, "I thought I'd discovered how a person can tell if he's found the right woman. You use logic, I thought. You lay out all the facts, see how they fit together. Sort of like designing a house, getting all the spaces right. But if there's one thing I should have realized by now, it's how much inspiration is involved, too. Inspiration...and love. I do love you, Toni. So much that it's making me crazy."

"Oh no," Toni said with a smile. "Don't tell me that. Because isn't that what Jackie and Hollan say? They drive each other crazy."

"Maybe they know something we don't." He kissed her again. He would have gone on kissing her, except that Marianne Shaw opened the door and peered at them.

"Well, it's about time *you* two came to your senses," she said. "But that doesn't solve the Jackie-and-Hollan problem. I checked home, and Jackie left a message on the answering machine. She said she couldn't possibly marry a man who would blow a gasket over the chocolate-covered cherry he'd just discovered under the seat of his car. She said it might sound insignificant, but little things lead to big things. Then she said not to worry—she was flying to Los Angeles on a last-minute news story." Marianne held up both hands in a gesture of utter frustration. "Not to *worry?*" she said. "I have a church crammed full of people, no bride and groom, and I'm not supposed to *worry?*"

The three of them considered the matter in silence. Then Kyle made up his mind.

"Shame to waste a whole wedding ceremony," he remarked. "Not to mention all that food at the reception."

Toni gave him a suspicious glance. "Kyle, what are you talking about?"

"I'm talking about asking you to marry me, Antonia—and I'm hoping this time you say yes."

"Yes," she said promptly. "But I don't think—"

"We get married right now," he said. "We forget about doing things in the logical order. Forget the engagement—just marry me now, Toni. I'll go from being the best man to being the groom. Tuxedo's the same, isn't it? We do it five minutes from now.''

She started to smile again, but then she shook her head. ''Some things *have* to be done in order,'' she said. ''We don't even have a license.''

''I happen to know some of the guests out there are your invitees,'' he said. ''Are you telling me at least one of them isn't a judge—somebody who can pull a few strings for us?''

''Judge Keller,'' said Marianne Shaw. ''Didn't you invite him, Toni?''

''Well, yes. I saw him sitting about the middle row, on the right side—''

''Be right back,'' Marianne said, disappearing.

Toni gazed at Kyle. Her face glowed, and she looked more beautiful than ever. ''Are we really going to do this?'' she asked breathlessly.

''I'm sure, Toni. Are you?''

''More sure,'' she said, ''than I've ever been of anything in my life.''

''No fears?'' he asked.

''No fears. They're gone. You took them away, Kyle.''

He contemplated his future bride. ''Hollan keeps acting like marriage means losing your freedom. Can't say I agree. Feels like I'm getting my freedom.''

She moved back into his arms. They were just getting started on another kiss when his future mother-in-law popped back in.

"All set," she announced. "Strings pulled. The judge made a phone call for the forms, and they should be here and signed by the time you say 'I do.' Save the mushy stuff for later, will you? Crowd's getting restless. They want a bride and groom—let's give them a bride and groom!"

A few minutes later, Kyle stood at the altar, watching as Toni walked down the aisle on the arm of her misty-eyed father. Maybe emerald green wasn't the traditional color of brides, but it suited her. If a few of the guests seemed a little puzzled, Kyle didn't pay much attention. He couldn't take his eyes off Toni.

She reached his side, and the organ music faded. Together they turned and faced the priest, who had risen admirably to the occasion. He even got their names right as he proceeded with the wedding ceremony.

"Do you, Kyle Brennan, take Antonia Shaw to be your lawfully wedded wife, to have and to hold..."

"I do."

"Do you, Antonia Shaw, take Kyle Brennan to be your lawfully wedded husband..."

"I do."

"You may now kiss the bride."

It was the moment he'd been waiting for. He took

Toni into his arms and kissed her thoroughly.
Toni...the love of his life.

TONI LIFTED HER ARMS and stretched luxuriously.
However, sharing a sleeping bag with her husband
made for confined space and she almost bumped
Kyle's nose. He opened his eyes.

"I need my sleep," he said, pretending to be
grouchy. "Honeymoons are exhausting."

"Don't I know it." She rolled over on top of him,
fitting her body to his. That was something they'd already had a lot of practice at in the past forty-eight
hours.

Morning sunlight streamed in through the windows
of the gray-shingle mansion. The island breeze was
cool, but promised to warm up. "So what'll it be today?" she asked. "More strolls on the beach? More
candy bars? Although I suppose we ought to eat something nutritious sooner or later."

"Make it later," he said, bringing his arms around
her and tracing his lips over her throat. "Toni..."

"Again?" she asked.

"I'm game, if you are."

"Oh...I'm game," she murmured.

Some time later, they lay in a tangle. Toni ran her
fingers over Kyle's chest.

"This island is going to keep you busy pretty
soon," she said. "But hopefully not too busy to over-

see the building of our house. You know…the one on Grandpa's land.''

He smoothed the tousled hair back from her face. ''That's tops on my list,'' he said. ''You and I need our weekend retreat.''

''Wow, that's a weekend retreat with bells on.''

''Then there's the house I have to design for us in Heritage City,'' he said. ''But we should probably keep the town house in San Francisco, too.''

''This is what happens when you're married to an architect,'' she said seriously. ''Suddenly you have more houses than you know what to do with.''

''We'll manage. Soon as I get my pilot's license, commuting back and forth will be no sweat. Thought we'd get a seaplane, too, for island hopping.''

It sounded like a wonderful future to Toni. But then she spied the heap of congratulatory telegrams on the floor. They'd been delivered from the mainland along with a replenishment of supplies, but Kyle and Toni had been too occupied to read them yet. Toni reached for one and tore it open. She scanned it as she snuggled against her husband.

''Hey, this one is from your parents,'' she said. ''And Aunt Eileen. She sounds a bit miffed that you got married without inviting her. Of course, she doesn't realize that we only had a five-minute engagement.'' Toni picked up another telegram, read it, and then sat up straight.

"Whoa," she said. "This is from Jackie and Hollan. Better have a look."

He took it from her and looked it over. "What do you know, they eloped. How about that. At least now they can wreak havoc as husband and wife. 'Cancún, Mexico—having a glorious time.' Cancún...I'd say that's more than a three-day honeymoon."

"So you're telling me that we went to all the trouble of finding them a honeymoon, and that's it? We have nothing to show for it?"

He traced a finger along her bare shoulder. "I'd say we have somethin' to show for it." His voice had that sexy hint of Texas. Toni never could resist Texas and California all rolled into one. She leaned down and kissed her husband.

"I love you, Kyle. Have I told you that recently?"

"I love you, too, Antonia. Forever."

"Forever," she agreed.

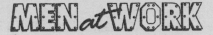

# MEN at WORK

## All work and no play?
## Not these men!

**July 1998**
### *MACKENZIE'S LADY by Dallas Schulze*

Undercover agent Mackenzie Donahue's
lazy smile and deep blue eyes were his best
weapons. But after rescuing—and kissing!—
damsel in distress Holly Reynolds, how could
he betray her by spying on her brother?

**August 1998**
### *MISS LIZ'S PASSION by Sherryl Woods*

Todd Lewis could put up a building with ease,
but quailed at the sight of a classroom! Still,
Liz Gentry, his son's teacher, was no battle-ax,
and soon Todd started planning some
extracurricular activities of his own....

**September 1998**
### *A CLASSIC ENCOUNTER*
### *by Emilie Richards*

Doctor Chris Matthews was intelligent, sexy
and *very* good with his hands—which made
him all the more dangerous to single mom
Lizette St. Hilaire. So how long could she
resist Chris's special brand of TLC?

Available at your favorite retail outlet!

## MEN AT WORK™

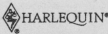

# Take 2 bestselling love stories FREE

## Plus get a FREE surprise gift!

## Special Limited-Time Offer

**Mail to Harlequin Reader Service®**

3010 Walden Avenue
P.O. Box 1867
Buffalo, N.Y. 14240-1867

**YES!** Please send me 2 free Harlequin Superromance® novels and my free surprise gift. Then send me 4 brand-new novels every month, which I will receive before they appear in bookstores. Bill me at the low price of $3.57 each plus 25¢ delivery and applicable sales tax, if any.* That's the complete price, and a saving of over 10% off the cover prices—quite a bargain! I understand that accepting the books and gift places me under no obligation ever to buy any books. I can always return a shipment and cancel at any time. Even if I never buy another book from Harlequin, the 2 free books and the surprise gift are mine to keep forever.

134 HEN CH7C

| | | |
|---|---|---|
| Name | (PLEASE PRINT) | |
| Address | | Apt. No. |
| City | State | Zip |

This offer is limited to one order per household and not valid to present Harlequin Superromance® subscribers. *Terms and prices are subject to change without notice. Sales tax applicable in N.Y.

USUP-98                                    ©1990 Harlequin Enterprises Limited

# HARLEQUIN SUPERROMANCE®

## GUARANTEED PAGE-TURNER!

# THE ENDS OF THE EARTH (#798)
## by Kay David

To protect her nephew, Eva Solis takes him and runs to a tiny village in the remotest part of Argentina. No one will find them—or so she thinks. Then a tall stranger arrives. And he seems to be watching her every move. Now Eva knows that the problem with running to the ends of the earth is there's nowhere else to go.

**Be sure to watch for this and other upcoming**
*Guaranteed Page-Turners!*

Available August 1998 wherever Harlequin books are sold.

# HARLEQUIN®
*Makes any time special* ™

# COMING NEXT MONTH

### #802 YOU WERE ON MY MIND • Margot Early
*The Midwives*

Ivy's a midwife; she understands the mystery of birth, the wonder of babies. But she hasn't got a baby of her own...has she? *She doesn't know.* Who was she before the accident, before she became Ivy? Then, unexpectedly, she learns that she was married and actually had a child, and she knows she has to go back to Tennessee, back to her family. *Even if she can't remember them...* The first book in Margot Early's stunning new trilogy, THE MIDWIVES.

### #803 CLASS ACT • Laura Abbot

"Is *this* all there is?" That's what Connie Weaver—teacher, divorced single parent and lone caregiver to her own elderly and difficult mother—wonders when she's presented with her fortieth birthday cake. Thanks to the demands of work and family, she doesn't have time for anything else, leaving her with only memories of the idyllic summer she spent with the one man who might've changed all that...and who's about to walk back into her life.

### #804 RIDE A PAINTED PONY • Carolyn McSparren
*Guaranteed Page-Turner*

*You never lose people on a carousel,* Nick Kendall tells Taylor Hunt. *They may go out of sight for a while, but they always come back.* His words are what Taylor is counting on as she and Nick are drawn into a world of intrigue, danger, betrayal and passion. *Ride A Painted Pony* by Carolyn McSparren will keep you on the edge of your seat. You may never look at a carousel in quite the same way again!

### #805 HOME TO STAY • Ann Evans

Fort Myers, Florida, simply isn't big enough for Abby MacAllister *and* Riley Kincaid. That's why it's been ten years since Abby's come home. But now she's back for a reason that has nothing to do with Riley. Maybe she won't run into him before she returns to Boston and her busy law practice. Fat chance! Because Riley Kincaid has moved into the house next door.